DIANA PALMER

RAGE OF
Passion

MIRA

MIRA

ISBN 1-55166-556-5

RAGE OF PASSION

Copyright © 1987 by Diana Palmer.

Visit us at www.mirabooks.com

Printed in U.S.A.

Tears stung her eyes.

It was fascinating that she could feel like this with him. She felt her own fingernails gripping the hard muscles of his upper arms, tugging gently. "Gabe," she whispered, giving in to the raging attraction.

"What did my mother offer you, Maggie?" he breathed against her mouth.

"Offer...me?" she whispered brokenly.

He moved closer, his legs suddenly trapping hers, his body demanding as his mouth hovered warmly over her lips. "She brought you down here for me. She's given up bringing me career girls, so now she's dredging up old memories. She wants me to marry you."

"Marry...you?" It was barely penetrating her hazy mind.

"Don't pretend," he said. His eyes were cold, not loverlike, as they met hers. "I heard you both plotting. Well, I'm not in the market for a wife, little Maggie," he said curtly. "But if you want to play around, I'm more than willing. You always did burn me up...."

"Nobody tops Diana Palmer...I love her stories."
—Jayne Ann Krentz

For my niece
Helen,
who sews a fine seam

Chapter One

The telegram crumpled in the slender hand, a scrap of badly used timber that would have served better as the tree it once was. Pale-green eyes stared down at it, hated it.

"Is it bad news, Mama?"

Becky's soft young voice broke through the anguish, brought her back to the reality of the huge empty Victorian house and the plain, withdrawn child.

"What, darling?" Her voice sounded odd. She cleared her throat and helplessly twisted the crumpled telegram in her hand. "Bad news? Well... yes."

Becky sighed. She was so old for six, Maggie sometimes thought. Her life had been disordered from the very beginning. An exclusive boarding school hadn't made her an extrovert; it had only emphasized her painful shyness, made it more obvious.

"Is it Daddy again?" Becky asked quietly. She read the answer in her mother's worried eyes and shrugged. "Well, Auntie Janet is coming today," she said with childlike enthusiasm and smiled. "That should make you feel better."

Margaret Turner smiled back. Her daughter's rare smiles were magic. "So she is, although she isn't really your aunt. She's my godmother. She and your Grandmother Turner were best friends. What a nice surprise for us, meeting her last week. She didn't even know I had you, you lovely little surprise, you."

Becky giggled—one of those sweet sounds that Maggie had heard so seldom lately. The boarding school was taking its toll on Becky, but there'd been no choice about it once Maggie went to work. She had no one to keep Becky after school, and her job meant occasional long hours and Saturday work. That left the child vulnerable, and Dennis wasn't above taking her away and hiding her somewhere. He was capable of anything where money was involved. And this newest threat, this telegram, made it plain that he was going to sue for full custody of Rebecca. He wanted Maggie to know immediately that he'd just given his lawyer the green light to go back to court.

Maggie swept back a strand of her short dark hair, which was very straight, curving into her high cheekbones. She was slender and tall, a good silhouette for the clothes that were such a rage this season. Not that she was buying new clothes. Thanks to her ex-husband's incredible alimony suit against her—which he'd won—and the fact that her attorneys were still draining her financially, times were getting harder by the day.

About all that was left was this white elephant they lived in and a relatively new car—and Becky's trust. Maggie's own father had never approved of her marriage to Dennis, although—at the time—she hadn't understood why. He'd cut Maggie out of his will entirely, leaving everything in trust for Becky. Maggie hadn't known this until his death, and she'd never forget the outburst from Dennis at the reading of the will. Her heart already broken, his callous attitude had taken the last of her spirit. After that, she hadn't really felt alive at all. She'd kept going for Becky's sake, not her own.

Dennis had tried to break the will. It couldn't be broken, but there were loopholes that would allow the administrator of the trust to sell stocks and bonds and reinvest them. Maggie could imagine what Dennis would do with that kind of control; in no time he'd have reduced Becky to poverty, robbed her of her inheritance.

As it was, Maggie was working long hours in a bookstore to make ends meet. She loved books, and the job was nice. But being without her daughter wasn't. She prayed for the day when she could bring Becky home and not have to worry that Dennis might kidnap her if she was left with a sitter. It was a good thing that Maggie didn't have a social life. But even in the days when her family had been wealthy and she'd had every advantage, she'd never cared for socializing. She'd kept to herself and avoided the fast crowds. She'd been much like Becky as a child—shy and introverted. She still was.

"I won't have to live with Daddy, will I?" Becky asked suddenly, and the look in her big eyes was poignant.

"Oh, darling, of course you won't!" Maggie drew the spindly-legged child close to her, caressing the incredibly thick hair that trailed down her daughter's ramrod-stiff back. Becky was all she had in the world now, the most precious thing she had left; the only thing of worth to come from the six-year marriage that she'd finally garnered enough courage to end just months before. The instant the divorce became final, she'd gone back to using her maiden name, Turner. She wanted nothing of Dennis in her life—not even his name.

"Never," Maggie added absently. "You won't have to live with him."

That might become a well-meant lie, she thought miserably as she cuddled her daughter, because Dennis was threatening to take Becky from her. They both knew that all he wanted was the mammoth trust Alvin Turner had set up for his grandchild before his death. Whoever had responsibility for Becky had access to that fortune. So far, Maggie had managed to keep the child out of her ex-husband's hands. He'd already announced his engagement to the woman he'd moved in with following the divorce, and Maggie's attorney was worried that Dennis might get the edge in a custody suit if he had a stable family life to offer little Rebecca.

Stability! If there was one thing Dennis Blaine didn't possess, it was stability. She should never have married him. She'd gone against her father's wishes, and against the advice of Aunt Janet. It had been a whirlwind courtship, and they'd made a handsome couple—the shy young debutante from San Antonio and the up-and-coming young salesman. Only after the wedding and her subsequent immediate pregnancy did Maggie learn that Dennis's main ambition was wealth, not a happy marriage. He liked women—and one wasn't enough. Barely three weeks after their wedding, he was having an affair with another woman, mostly as an act of vengeance against Maggie, who'd refused to stake him in a get-rich-quick scheme he'd concocted.

She sighed over her daughter's silky hair. Dennis, she'd discovered, had a vindictive nature, and it had grown worse as time passed. His affairs were legion. She'd tried to leave him, and he'd beaten her up. It was the first and last time. She'd threatened to go to the police, with all the scandal that would have raised, and he'd promised in tears never to do it again. But there were other ways he'd been able to get back at her, especially after Becky came along. More than once he'd threatened to abduct the child and hide her if Maggie didn't go along with his demands for more money.

In the end, it had been because of Dennis that she'd moved out and filed for divorce. Dennis had brought one of his lady loves into the house and had been cavorting with her in bed when Becky had come home unexpectedly and found them. Dennis had threatened Becky, warning her not to téll what she'd seen. But Becky was spunky. She had told. And that very day, Maggie had moved with the child back to her old family home in San

Antonio. Thank God her parents had held on to the house even after they'd moved to Austin.

Dennis, meanwhile, had cut his losses and stayed in Austin, where he and Maggie had lived together for the six years of their disastrous marriage. Once the divorce had become final, he'd initiated a grueling lawsuit—with Maggie's money, ironically enough—and had ultimately been granted visitation rights.

Well, she wasn't giving up her child to that money-grubbing opportunist. She said so, frequently. But Dennis's forthcoming remarriage could cause some devilish problems. She didn't quite know what to do, how to handle this new development.

"Couldn't we run away?" Becky asked as she drew back. "We could go live with Aunt Janet and her family, couldn't we? They own a real ranch, and Aunt Janet's so nice. She said after she visits us, we could visit her and ride horses—"

"I'm afraid we can't do that," Maggie said quickly, forcing down the image of Gabriel Coleman that swam with sickening intensity before her eyes. He frightened her, colored her dreams, even though it had been years since she'd seen him. Even now, she could close her eyes, and there he was. Big, lean, rawhide tough. All man. Dennis wouldn't dare threaten her around Gabe, but Maggie was too frightened of him to ask for sanctuary. It was a well-known fact that Janet and her son didn't get along. Maggie had enough problems already without adding Gabe's antagonism to them. He didn't care for her. He thought of her as a bored socialite; he always had. She was prejudged and predamned in his pale eyes. She'd never stood a chance with him, even in her younger days. He hadn't given her a second look. Once, she'd wanted him to. But after Dennis, she'd had too many scars for another relationship. Especially with a man like Gabriel, who was so much a man.

"But why can't we?" Becky persisted, all eyes—green eyes, like her mother's.

"Because I have a job," Maggie said absently, smoothing the long silky hair of the little girl. "Well, except for this month-long vacation I'm getting while Trudie is in Europe. She owns the shop, you see." Trudie had decided that Maggie needed some time off, too, and she'd closed up shop despite the loss of cash. It was one of many reasons that Maggie loved her friend so much.

"Then can't we go home with Aunt Janet? Oh, can't we?" Becky pleaded, all but jumping up and down in her enthusiasm.

"No, and you mustn't ask her, either," Maggie said shortly. "Anyway, you have one more week at school before vacation. You have to go back and finish out the semester.''

"Yes, Mama," Becky sighed, giving in without a fight.

"Good girl. Suppose you dash out to the kitchen and remind Mary that we're to have an apple pie tonight in Aunt Janet's honor," she added with a smile.

"Yes, Mama," Becky agreed, brightening. She ran, skirts flying, out of the immaculate living room with its wing chairs and Chippendale sofa—beautiful relics of a more graceful age—down the long hall toward the spacious kitchen.

The house had been in Maggie's family for eighty years or more. It was here that she and Dennis had spent an occasional weekend with her mother after her father's death from a heart attack, but she didn't mind the memories as much as she would have minded losing the homeplace. She touched the arm of the sofa lovingly. Her mother had sat here in happier days, doing embroidery, while her father had sprawled in the big armchair on his visits home—and they'd been few, those last years, because as an ambassador his duty had kept him away.

Maggie's mother had traveled with him until ill health had forced her to remain in Texas. She'd died within six months of her tragic loss, swiftly following the husband she'd adored. Maggie often thought that such love was a rare thing. Certainly she hadn't found it in her marriage. She wondered if she ever would find it. She was much too frightened to take the chance a second time; the risk, to Becky, was even greater than the risk to herself.

She studied her slender hands quietly, drinking in the subtle scent of lavender that clung like dust to the old furniture. A knock on the door disturbed her thoughts, then the knob twisted and Janet Coleman breezed in.

"Darling! Oh, it's so hot outside! Why I keep an apartment in San Antonio I don't know, when I could have gone someplace cold."

Like a white-haired whirlwind, Janet embraced the younger, taller woman with a deep sigh.

"You must love the city; you've had that apartment ever since I can remember." Maggie smiled, drawing back to stare down at the older woman in the chic gray suit.

"I've got my nerve, haven't I, inviting myself for dinner." Janet laughed. "But I couldn't resist it. It's been so many years, and to run into you out of the blue in that department store! Shocking, to think I didn't even know about Becky! And here you'd been married for six years, and getting a divorce…" She shook her head. "I miss your mother so much. I have no one to talk to these days, with the girls away from home and Gabe so business oriented. And,'' she added quietly, ''I'm hardly ever at the ranch these days myself. I've been in Europe for the past seven months.''

Maggie had gone to boarding school with the girls, Audrey and Robin—the same school, in fact, that Becky was in now.

''Audrey is living with a man in Chicago,'' Janet said, exasperated. She flushed a little at Maggie's pointed stare. ''Yes, that's what I said. Isn't it outrageous? I know it's the in thing to do these days, but honestly, Maggie, I had to stop Gabriel from getting the next train up there. He was all for putting a bullet in the man. You know Gabe.''

Maggie nodded. Yes, that was Gabe all right. His answer to most things was physical. She trembled a little with inner reaction to him—a reaction that had always been there, but one she'd never really understood.

''I talked him out of it, but he's still simmering.'' She shuddered delicately. ''I just hope Audrey has the good sense to stay away until he cools down. He'd have them married at gunpoint.''

''Yes, I don't doubt it. How's Robin?'' she added with a smile, because she liked Janet's younger daughter.

''She's still trying to be an oil rigger.'' Janet

shook her head. "She says it's what she wants to do."

"Times have changed, Janet." Maggie laughed. "Women are taking over the world."

"Please don't say that in front of Gabe," the older woman murmured dryly. "He doesn't like the modern world."

"Neither do I, at times." Maggie sighed. She stared at Janet. "Is he still ranching?"

"With a vengeance. It's roundup time, darling." Janet laughed. "He doesn't speak to anyone for days during roundup. He's hardly even home anymore. He has board meetings and buying trips and selling trips and seminars, and he sits on the boards of God knows how many corporations and colleges and banks... Even when I'm home, he never listens to me."

"Does he know about Becky and me?" she wondered aloud.

"I've mentioned your mother over the years," Janet said. "But no, I don't suppose I've had a lot to say about you. He's so touchy when I mention women, I've given up trying. I did find this lovely girl and I brought her out to the ranch to meet him." Janet flushed. "It was terrible." She shook her head. "Since then, I've decided that it's better if I let him lead his own life. So I don't mention anybody to him. Especially eligible women," she added with a pert laugh.

Maggie shook her head. "Well, he'd never have to worry about me. I'm off men for life!"

"I can understand why," Janet muttered. "I never liked that man. He smiled too much."

This from a woman whose son was a caveman... But Maggie wasn't going to remark on that. She had no use at all for that kind of man. She'd had enough of being afraid and dominated and intimidated. No man was ever going to get the chance to do to her what Dennis had. Not ever again.

"If only Gabe would get married," Janet said. And there was such bitter remorse in her voice. "He never had the chance to do the things that most young men do. I feel responsible for that, sometimes." The remorse in the tired old voice made Maggie feel sympathetic.

She knew about Janet's family, of course. Janet and her own mother had been best friends for years, and Maggie had learned things about the other family, especially the only son, that she wished she could forget. Janet's girls had been spoiled rotten by two doting parents, and that hadn't helped. After Jonathan Coleman's death, Audrey had run wild and Robin had gone off to college. Gabe was left at the head of the massive ranch holding—with no help at all from his family, none of whom knew anything about business.

Gabe had shouldered the burden, though, and that strong back had never bent in all the years since. Maggie had always admired his strength. He was unique. A pioneer with a rugged spirit and a savage determination to persevere.

"Here's my Becky," Janet gushed, opening her arms to the little girl, who darted into them with unabashed affection.

"Oh, Auntie Janet, I'm so glad you came," Becky enthused. Becky had taken instantly to the older woman during that chance meeting, and when she'd learned that Maggie was Janet's goddaughter, she'd "adopted" herself as Janet's niece. Maggie hadn't fussed, and Janet had been delighted. The poor child had no other living relatives, except her terror of a father.

Becky hugged the old lady tightly, her eyes closed. She drew back a long minute later. "My daddy is trying to make me come and live with him, and I told Mama we should run away, but she won't."

Janet darted a searching glance at Maggie, who was standing red-faced in the center of the kitchen while old Mary gaped briefly at the small group before ambling back to her teacakes and silverware. Mary had been with the family since Maggie was a child. She didn't work for them full-time anymore but only came in when she needed a little extra money—and Maggie often worked overtime to provide that money, to help the woman who'd been so much a part of her childhood.

"So that's still going on, is it?" Janet asked haughtily. "Really, dear, you should let me ask Gabriel to speak to Dennis. He wouldn't mind."

Maggie could just imagine Gabriel doing anything for her. It was whimsical. She shrugged. "My attorneys are handling it, but thank you for the offer."

"I feel guilty. I've lost touch with you all since you moved to Austin," Janet said. "If it hadn't been for our chance meeting downtown, I wouldn't have invited myself to visit you."

"You know you're always welcome here," Maggie chided.

Janet searched her face quietly. "I've been away too long, haven't I, dear? I should have been keeping an auntly eye on you." She shook her head. "I lose track of things these days. Absentmindedness, I suppose. I remembered after I ran into you that I hadn't ever mentioned your marriage to the girls; that's how terrible I am."

"We haven't seen each other in a long time," Maggie reminded her with a smile. "But it's so nice to have you here." She led Janet down into the dining room, where the older woman sat down at the cherrywood table, fanning herself with her hand. "Darling, it's so hot, even for spring. However do you stand it?"

"I'll get you a fan," Becky volunteered, and opened the buffet drawer, pulling out a large wooden fan with a beautiful spring scene on one side and the name of a local funeral parlor in huge black letters on the other.

Janet smiled appreciatively at her and began to fan herself furiously. "If you only had air conditioning." She shook her head. "We had to put it in two years ago. The heat is getting more unbearable every year."

Becky seated herself primly in a chair beside Janet while Mary bustled around serving teacakes and steaming cups of freshly brewed tea. Afterward, Becky was sent out to play and Mary went into the kitchen to finish dinner and watch the little girl out the back window.

"Now," Janet said firmly, transfixing Maggie with those piercing light eyes. "Let's hear it all."

Maggie knew she had no choice, so she told her godmother everything. It felt good to get it off her chest. It had been so long since she'd had anybody she could talk to.

Janet listened, only occasionally asking questions. When Maggie had finished, she stared into her teacup for a minute, then spoke. "Come home with me," she said, looking up. "You need a little time away, to think things through. The ranch is the perfect refuge—and the one place Dennis won't come looking for you."

That was true enough. Dennis, like Maggie, had heard plenty about Gabriel Coleman, and Dennis wasn't suicidal.

"But what about Becky?" Maggie asked. "I can't take her out of school now...."

"We'll come back for her week after next," Janet assured her. "She's in boarding school, darling; they won't let Dennis have her without a court order. She'll be safe."

Maggie fingered her cup with a sigh. It sounded like heaven—to get away from the city, to be able to think in placid surroundings. If only it weren't for Gabriel...

Memories of him had colored her young life for years. He was stamped permanently on her thoughts like an indelible ink. She knew so much about him. Like the time he'd forced some rustlers off the road into a ditch and held the three men with a shotgun until one of his hands got the sheriff there. Then there was the knock-down-drag-out fight with one of his men right in the street.

Maggie had actually witnessed that. Sometimes she wondered if it hadn't happened because of her.

She'd been spending a couple of weeks with his sisters at the ranch when she was about sixteen. They'd gone into town with Janet to shop, driven by one of the hands, a new man with too interested eyes and a way of talking to the young girls that amused Robin and Audrey but terrified Maggie. Gabe had been at the hardware store, right next door to the grocery store where Janet shopped. And when the girls had come out, the new man had put his hand on Maggie's waist and insolently let it drop to her hip in a blatant caress.

Gabe had moved over a rack of shovels with alarming speed, and his powerful fists had made a shuddering mess of the new cowhand. Gabe had fired him on the spot, oblivious to the fascinated stares of passersby, and in language that had colored Maggie's face a bright red.

Gabe had started to move toward her, and with visible apprehension she'd backed away from him, her green eyes wide and frightened. Whatever he'd meant to say never got said. He'd glared at the girls and demanded to know what they were staring at. Then he'd ordered them back to the car and stalked off, lighting a cigarette as calmly as if nothing had happened. The girls had said later that he'd explained the man had gotten in trouble for mistreating an animal. But Maggie had always wondered if it hadn't been because he'd insulted her. It was one of those unfinished episodes that haunted her.

Maybe it had all happened a long time ago, she conceded. Still... Memories were one thing, but living under his roof was quite another. And she definitely preferred to keep Gabe at a safe distance. Like the distance from San Antonio to the Coleman ranch.

But saying no to Janet Coleman was like talking to a wall. Within minutes, Maggie found herself agreeing to the visit.

Chapter Two

If Maggie had thought Janet would just go back home and leave Maggie to follow, she was dead wrong. Janet helped her pack and even drove them to the exclusive boarding school to drop Becky off and tell the office where Maggie could be reached if she was needed.

Mrs. Haynes, who ran the school, was a good friend of the family. It was comforting to Maggie to know that the woman was aware of the situation with Dennis and knew not to let him take the child. She still felt uneasy about leaving Becky, but she needed time to think and plan. If she was to keep her daughter, she had to act quickly.

"I hate leaving you here," Maggie told the child

as she hugged her goodbye. "Becky, I promise you, as soon as school is out, we'll make some better arrangements, so that you can stay with me all the time."

"You mustn't worry, Mama," Becky said seriously, sounding for all the world like an adult. "I'll be just fine. And as soon as school is out, you come right back here and get me, all right?"

"All right, darling," Maggie promised, smothering an amused smile. "I will. Be a good girl."

Minutes later, Maggie and Janet were on their way to the massive ranch the Colemans owned, which was far to the north of San Antonio, up near Abilene. The nearest town was Junction, a modern little place with just enough stores to qualify for a post office. It even had an airport of sorts.

"I'm sorry I couldn't get Gabriel to fly me here," Janet apologized as they sped up the long highway in the sleek silver Lincoln Mark IV that was the older woman's pride and joy. "But he was busy with roundup and couldn't be bothered," she muttered darkly. "After all, I'm just his mother. Why should I come before the cattle? He couldn't even get a good price for me; I'm too old and tough!"

It was all Maggie could do to keep from laughing. Janet had a dry sense of humor and she was delightful as a companion. Yes, maybe this would turn out for the best after all. It was going to be a nice visit, and she'd be able to put Dennis and the horror of the past into perspective and plan her strategy to keep Becky out of her ex-husband's clutches. If only it weren't for Gabriel...

It was spring and already hot in this part of the world, and the ride was tiring despite the air conditioning and the car's luxurious interior. Janet had to stop frequently for gas and soft drinks and rest rooms. But eventually they passed through the edges of the beautiful hill country, nearing Abilene, and brush turned to lush, cultivated flatland.

"We have two airplanes, after all," Janet continued her chatter as they drove the final few miles. "Not to mention a helicopter." She glanced at Maggie. "You're worn out, aren't you, dear?" She sighed.

"No, not at all," Maggie said gently, and even managed to laugh. It had been a long time since she'd felt like laughing, but there was something very relaxing about Janet's company. "We've seen some beautiful country, and I'm really kind of glad we did it this way. You're tired though, aren't you?" she probed gently.

"Me?" the older woman scoffed. "My dear, in

my youth, I could break wild horses. I'm a Texan."

So was Maggie, and the girl she'd been would have gloried in the challenge of a wild horse. But so much of the spirit had been drained out of her in the past few years. If it hadn't been for Becky, she wasn't sure how long she could have kept her sanity under that kind of pressure.

"I hope you're going to enjoy the ranch," Janet was murmuring as she pulled off onto a graveled road with a huge sign near it that read, "Coleman Ranch, Purebred Santa Gertrudis Cattle."

"I know I will," Maggie promised. She smiled at the sight of the big red-coated cattle grazing behind rugged, rustic fences. "Santa Gertrudis is the only native American breed, isn't it?" she murmured knowledgeably. "Founded on the King Ranch and now famous all over the world. They're so beautiful.... Oh, what I wouldn't give for some of my own!"

Janet drew in a deep breath, her gaze wistful. "Oh, my dear, if only I'd brought you here sooner..." She shook her head as she turned back to the road and eased the car forward. "It's so ironic. Gabriel is obsessed with cattle. You'd have made the perfect daughter-in-law."

"No matchmaking," Maggie cautioned, feeling

herself go taut with apprehension. "With all due respect to your son, the last thing in the world I want is a domineering man in my life again. Okay?"

Janet smiled gently. "Okay. And I wouldn't do that to you, truly. But you are so special, my dear."

She smiled back. "You're pretty special yourself." She glanced toward the big white clapboard house with its graceful long porches and green shutters. It had a faintly colonial look about it, but without the huge columns. There were wicker chairs all over, a big porch swing, and flowers blooming in wild profusion everywhere. It was spectacular.

"It's about the same size as your own, isn't it?" Janet laughed. "My father built it with no particular style in mind. It often draws comment for that."

"It's lovely," Maggie sighed. She glanced toward the long wire fences, frowning. "I expected white fences," she murmured.

Her companion laughed. "Gabriel is tight with a dollar," she teased. "There are hundreds of acres of land here, and fencing is expensive. Especially electric fences, which are all he uses these days. He cuts costs wherever he can. Actually," she added, "it's a full-time job just keeping track of cattle and keeping rustlers out. We only keep purebreds here, and when a bull can bring as much as half a million dollars, you can understand why Gabriel is so careful about security. He had a man full-time to do nothing but maintain security here."

"Good heavens" Maggie exclaimed. "People still rustle cattle?"

"Yes, they do. They come in big trucks; it's been modernized along with cattle ranching, but rustling is still a problem."

"I wouldn't have guessed," Maggie said as Janet pulled up to the steps and stopped. She barely noticed Janet's sudden stiffening or the disturbed look in her eyes; she was too busy watching the man who was approaching the stopped car.

He was tall. Lithe and lean, he walked with an arrogance that immediately put Maggie's back up. He was dressed like a working cowboy, but he moved like no other man she'd ever seen. He was graceful, from the top of his wide-brimmed tan hat to the toes of his worn, warped boots. His dusty leather batwing chaps were flying with the sharp movements of long, powerfully muscled legs, and what she could see of his darkly tanned face under his hat wasn't at all welcoming.

He paused beside the car, and Janet rushed out with an exclamation of pleasure to hug him with the enthusiasm and warmth that seemed so much a part of her. But he drew back sharply.

"For God's sake, stop that!" he bit off, grimacing. He held his side and caught his breath with a hot curse. "I've been bitten by a rattlesnake. The arm's still swollen, and it'll be days before I can get back to work. I don't need it broken!"

Janet flushed, looking flustered and taken aback. "I'm sorry, dear..."

"I can't ride a horse, can't bounce around in the damned trucks, I can't even fly the plane!" He glared at Janet as if it were all her fault. "Landers is even having to drive me around. I've been sicker than an overfed dog."

"I...I'm sorry. You do look pale," Janet said uneasily. "It must be painful."

"I'll live." He looked past Janet to the younger woman, and his chin lifted, his eyes narrowing. He scowled thoughtfully as Maggie stepped from the car, and she saw his eyes under the shadowy brim of the hat.

She was tempted to turn around and run. It was that kind of look. There was nothing welcoming in his lean, sharp-featured countenance. He had a crook in the middle of his nose, as if somebody had broken it. His black eyebrows were as shaggy and thick as the hair on his head, and his protruding brow shadowed eyes as light as candles, as penetrating as only blue eyes could be. His high cheekbones ran down to a firm, hard-looking mouth over a stubborn chin. He wasn't a handsome man, although his face had character and his body was as sensuously powerful as that of a movie star. The fabric of her dreams—in the flesh. But it was no surprise to Maggie that he was thirty-eight and unmarried. It would take a strong woman, a fiery woman, for a man like that. She felt cold chills at the thought of what he might expect of a woman in intimacy.

The feeling must have been mutual, because the look he was giving her spoke volumes. She could imagine how citified she must seem to him, in her lacy white blouse and white slacks, with dainty strapped sandals. She should have worn jeans, she thought belatedly, as she'd planned to in the beginning. Why had she dressed up so? She needed this vacation so badly, and here she'd gone and antagonized him at first glance.

"Gabe, you remember Mary's daughter, Maggie Turner, don't you?" Janet asked.

Maggie stared up at him, watching the fleeting

lift of his eyebrows. He looked at her with cold disinterest. "I remember her."

"It's nice to...see you again," she faltered.

He nodded, but he didn't return the greeting. He dismissed her without a second thought and turned back to his mother impatiently as a truck with the ranch logo purred to a stop nearby. "I won't be gone long, but I'm expecting an important call from Cheyenne. If it comes through while I'm gone, have the party call back at five."

"Certainly, dear," Janet agreed. "I'm sorry if I've...we've come at a bad time..."

"Don't you always, Mother?" he asked with a cold smile. "Isn't Europe more your style than dust and cattle?"

"I came to see you," the older woman said with quiet pride.

"I'll be back directly." He turned without another glance and walked to the truck, grimacing despite his iron control as he climbed inside the cab and managed to close the door, waving away the cowboy who offered to help him. They drove off in a cloud of dust.

Janet sighed half-angrily. "I'll never understand him," she said under her breath. "I didn't raise him without manners. I'm sorry, Maggie."

"There's no need to apologize," Maggie said quietly. "I gather that he's in some pain."

"And irritable at having to stay at home when there's work to be done. Roundup is a bad time for everyone. Besides that," she said miserably, "he doesn't like it when I come here. I have to confess that I needed you as much as you needed the rest. I don't like having to cope by myself. But truly, you'll enjoy it. He won't be around much," she added with a hopeful look. "Just until his arm will let him get back to work. Knowing my son," she added bitterly, "it shouldn't take more than a couple of days. Nothing keeps him down for long. He'll convince the doctor that strapping it will accomplish miracles."

"He isn't the most welcoming man," Maggie murmured.

"He'll be gone before you know it. Now come on and let's get settled in," Janet said firmly. "This is my home, too—even if I'm not allowed to visit it very often!"

Maggie didn't reply. She wasn't sure that she'd done the right thing in coming. Gabriel was stone-cold hateful, and time hadn't improved his old dislike of her. She knew instinctively that if his mother hadn't been around, he'd have packed her right back to San Antonio. It wasn't the brightest beginning.

She spent the next two hours reacquainting herself with the big house and getting to know the new cook and housekeeper, whose name was Jennie. She was small and dark and gay, and Maggie liked her immediately.

She settled in, changing her white outfit for jeans and a yellow blouse. She brushed her short hair toward her face and hoped that her appearance wouldn't antagonize the cattleman any further when she went down to have supper with the family.

Gabriel was already at the table, looking furious and glaring at her the minute she walked into the spacious, elegant dining room. In fact, his look was so accusatory that she froze in the doorway, flashing on a line from a dog-training manual about not showing fear and making no sudden moves. Perhaps it would work with the half-civilized cattleman whose mother was obviously kicking him under the table.

"Do join us, dear," Janet said with a glare toward her taciturn son.

"I'm sorry if I've held you up," Maggie said gently, seating herself on the other side of Janet for protection with a wary, green-eyed glance at Gabe that seemed to amuse him.

"Dinner is promptly at six," he returned with a lifted eyebrow. "I don't like being held up, in case you've forgotten." She started to speak, but he cut her off with a lifted hand, ignoring his mother's seething irritation to add mockingly, "I don't bite, Miss Turner," his voice deep and faintly amused.

"Could I have that in writing, please?" she asked with a nervous laugh. She smiled at Janet. "The air smells so fresh and clean out here. No exhaust fumes!"

"That's right, city girl," Gabe replied. He leaned back carefully, favoring his right side, with his coffee cup in his lean hand. He wasn't even neatly dressed or particularly cleaned up. He was still wearing his work clothes, except that his dusty shirt was open halfway down his tanned chest, where a wedge of thick black hair arrowed toward his wide leather belt. That disturbed Maggie, just as it had in her teens, and she looked down at her plate, fiddling with putting the napkin in her lap.

"I would have cleaned up," he said unexpectedly, a bite in his slow drawl as he obviously mistook her expression for distaste, "but I'd just come in from the holding pens when I went to the doctor, and I'm a bit tired."

Her eyes came up quickly, with an apology in them. "Mr. Coleman, this is your home," she said gently. "I wouldn't be so rude as to criticize how you dress."

He stared at her calculatingly for a long moment—so long that she dropped her gaze again to her plate. Finally, he reached for the platter of beef and helped himself, to his mother's obvious relief.

"How did you get bitten, darling?" Janet asked him.

"I reached for a rope without looking."

Janet gnawed her lip. "It must be painful. You won't be able to work for a few days, I guess."

He gave her a cold stare. "I'm managing. If I felt a little stronger, I could ride. It's just the swelling and the pain, that's all. I won't be stuck here for long, I hope."

Janet started to make a comment, but she forced herself to remain silent. It did no good to argue with him.

He glanced from her to Maggie as he buttered a huge fluffy biscuit. "What are you doing these days?" he asked curiously.

"Me? I'm working at a bookstore," Maggie told him. She glanced up and down again, hating the surge of heat to her face. He had the most incredible effect on her, even after the anguish of her marriage.

"Working, did you say?" His light eyes lifted and probed hers like a microscope. "Your people were wealthy."

"Times change," she said quietly. "I'm not wealthy now. I'm just a working girl."

"Have some peas, dear." Janet tried to interrupt.

He put the biscuit down and cocked his head, studying her with narrowed eyes. "It shows," he said absently. "You don't look like the spunky little kid who used to play with my sisters. What's happened to you?"

Maggie felt herself going cold. He was watching her, like a cat watching a mouse. She felt vulnerable and a little afraid of that single-mindedness. Once, she would have taken exception to his blunt challenge. But there had been so many fights, so much struggle. Her spirit was carefully buried— had to be, for Becky's sake.

She laid down her fork and stared at him. "I've grown up," she replied, her voice soft.

His level gaze sized her up. "You had money. And now you don't. Then what brings you here, Miss Turner? Are you looking for a vacation or a man to support you?"

"Gabriel!" Janet slammed her napkin down. "How dare you!"

Maggie clasped her hands tightly under the table and stared at him with a courage she didn't really feel. "Your mother offered me a visit, Mr. Coleman," she said dully. "I needed to get away for a little while, that's all. You'll have to excuse me for being so dim, but I didn't realize that I needed your permission as well as Janet's. If you want me to leave…?" She started to rise.

"Oh, for God's sake, sit down," he snapped. His eyes cut into hers. "The last thing I need is a Texas society girl out here at roundup, but if Mother wants you, you're welcome. Just keep to the house," he warned softly, his eyes emphasizing the threat. "And out of my way."

He tossed his own napkin down, ignoring his mother's furious glare.

"I won't get in your way," Maggie said, her voice, her whole manner vulnerable.

Gabriel's pale eyes narrowed as he bent his dark head to light a cigarette, watching her the whole time. "Won't you? What a difference," he added as he took a draw from the cigarette. "The girl I remember was like a young filly, all long legs and excitement and blushing fascination. How you've changed, Maggie Turner."

The comment surprised her. She looked up, feeling hot all over as his eyes searched hers. "You haven't," she blurted out. "You're just as blunt and rude and overbearing as you ever were."

He actually grinned. "Just as mean-tempered, too, honey. So look out," he added as he got to his feet. He groaned a little with the movement and murmured a curse under his breath.

"Can I get you anything?" Janet asked, frowning.

He spared her a cool glance. "Nothing, thank you," he replied formally. He nodded at the women, the brief and unexpected humor gone as he turned and went out the door.

"I'm sorry," Janet told Maggie. "It's roundup, you know. He gets so ill-tempered, and he doesn't really like women very much."

"He doesn't like me very much, you mean," Maggie said quietly, staring at the tablecloth. "He never did." She smiled wistfully. "Do you know, I once had the most terrible crush on him. He never found out, thank goodness, and I outgrew it. But I used to think he was the whole world."

"And now?" Janet queried gently.

Maggie bit her lower lip and laughed, the sound soft and nervous. "Now, I think I'm a little afraid of him. I'm not sure that coming here was a good idea.''

"Oh, yes, it was," Janet said. "I'm certain that it will work out. You'll see. I've got it all planned."

Maggie didn't ask what "it" was, but the man listening outside the door had a face that would have stopped traffic. He'd read an entirely different meaning into Janet's innocent remark, and he was livid with anger. So his mother was matchmaking again. This time she'd picked a woman he knew, although she couldn't know what he'd thought of Maggie Turner. His eyes narrowed. Well, this time his mother had gone too far. And if little Maggie thought she was going to lead him down the aisle, she had a surprise coming. A big one!

He went out the door, his eyes cold with calculation, his steps so soft that no one heard him leave.

Janet shook her head. "I was so sure that he wouldn't be around the house," she said. "He's hurting, but he won't admit it; that's why he was so rude.''

"Is he like that with all women?" she probed gently.

Janet picked up a roll and buttered it carefully. "I'll tell you about it, one day," she said quietly, her eyes sad. "For now, let's just say that he had a particularly bad experience, and it was my fault. I've been trying to make it up to him ever since. And failing miserably."

"Can't you talk to him about it?" Maggie asked.

Janet only laughed. "Gabriel has a habit of walking off when he doesn't want to hear me. He won't listen. I tried, once, to explain what happened. He cut me dead and went to Oklahoma on a business trip. After that…well, I suppose I just lost my nerve. My son can be very intimidating."

"I remember," came the dry reply.

Janet smiled at her. "Yes. You understand, don't you? You know, I never even told him that you'd married. He had an odd way of ignoring me if I mentioned you, after that summer you spent some time here. You remember, when he had the fight in town with that cowboy…?"

Maggie actually blushed and couldn't hide it from Janet. "Oh, yes. How could I forget?"

"He wouldn't talk about you at all after that. He seemed preoccupied for a long time, and a little strange, in fact," she mused. "He filled in our swimming pool and wouldn't let anyone ride Butterball…"

Something barely remembered, exciting, stirred

deep inside Maggie. He'd given her Butterball to ride, and she could still see him towering over her, his lean hands working with the cinch. She'd adored him in those days, despite his evident antagonism toward her. Even that was inexplicable, because he got along well with most women. He was polite and courteous to everyone—except Maggie.

"He's still not pleased to have me around," Maggie murmured.

"Well, it's my home, too," Janet said doggedly. "And I love having you here. Do have some more beef. It's our own, you know."

"Purebred Santa Gertrudis?" Maggie exclaimed in horror, staring blankly at the platter Janet was offering her.

"What?" Then Janet got the message and laughed. "No, no, dear. Gabriel raises some beef cattle as well. Purebred...oh, that's sinfully amusing. Gabriel would eat his horse before he'd eat one of the purebreds. Here, have a roll to go with it. Jennie bakes them fresh every day."

Maggie took one, savoring it, and not for the first time she had misgivings about the wisdom of coming here. Gabriel seemed to be out for blood, and she wondered if the Coleman ranch wasn't going to become a combat zone.

Chapter Three

It *was* vaguely like living in a war zone, Maggie thought as the first few days went by. Gabriel was impatient and irritable because of his arm, and he seemed to hate the whole world. Nothing pleased him—least of all, it appeared, having Maggie in the house. He treated her with a cold formality that raised goose bumps on her arms. It was obvious that he was tolerating her for his mother's sake alone. And just in case she hadn't already guessed it on her own, he spelled it out for her at breakfast three days after she'd arrived.

He glanced up coldly when she sat down. It was just the two of them, because his mother was still upstairs. She and Maggie had been up late talking the night before, and Janet seemed to sleep poorly anyway.

"I'm sorry, am I late?" she asked, throwing out a white flag.

He smoked his cigarette quietly, his icy eyes level and cutting. "Do you care, one way or another?" he asked.

She took a deep breath. "I realize you don't want me here..."

"That's an understatement." He rolled the cigarette between his lean, dark fingers while he studied her. "What did she offer you to get you down here, Margaret?" he added suddenly, using her name for the first time since she'd been at the ranch.

Her eyes widened. "N-nothing," she stammered. "I just needed some rest, that's all."

"Rest from what?" he persisted. His pale eyes cut into hers. "You're thin. You always were, but not like this. You're pale, too, and you look unwell. What's going on, Margaret? What are you running from? And why run to me?"

Her face went white. She caught her breath. "As if I would, *ever*, run to you...!"

"Don't be insulting." He lifted the cigarette to his chiseled lips, watching her. "Talk to me."

She was closing up, visibly, her body taut with nerves. "I can't."

"You won't," he corrected. He smiled slowly, but it wasn't a pleasant smile. It was impatient and half-angry. "I'm not blind. I know my mother, I know how her mind works. You're the sacrifice, I gather. Are you a willing one, I wonder?"

"I don't understand," she said, bewildered.

"You will," he promised, making a threat of the words. He got to his feet, more easily now than he had three days ago. He was improving rapidly; he even looked better.

"I came to visit with Janet—not to get in your way, Gabriel," she tried one last time, hating her lack of spirit.

Gabriel seemed frozen in place. It was the first time she'd said his name since she arrived. He looked at her and felt a wave of heat hit him like a whirlwind in the chest. Odd, how it had always disturbed him to look at her, to be around her. She got under his skin. And now it was worse, now that she was vulnerable. It irritated him to see her like this and not know why. Was it an act? Was it part of the plan his mother had mentioned when she'd thought he was out of earshot? He was wary of the whole damned situation, and the way Maggie affected him after all these years was the last straw.

"In my way, or in my bed, Maggie?" he asked, deliberately provoking. "Because you wanted me when you were sixteen. I knew it, felt it when you looked at me. Do you still want me, honey?"

Her face paled, and she dropped her eyes to her faded jeans, staring dully at her slender hands. The old Maggie would have snapped back at him. But the old Maggie was dead, a casualty of her marriage to a cruel and brutal man. She felt sick all over.

"Don't," she whispered, closing her eyes. "Don't."

"Look at me!" He stared down at her with his cold blue eyes until she obeyed him. Dimly, she noticed he was wearing jeans and a long-sleeved chambray shirt with worn, warped leather boots. In one lean, strong hand, a battered gray Stetson dangled. "You and Mother don't have a chance in hell of pulling it off," he said quietly. "Give it up. I don't want to hurt you."

And with that enigmatic statement, he turned and strode angrily out the door.

She didn't tell Janet about the confrontation. And afterward, she made it her business to be where he wasn't. He glared at her as if he hated

her very presence, but she pretended not to notice.
And around his mother, at least, he was courteous
enough in his cold way.

She wondered if he'd ever loved anyone or been
loved. He seemed so unapproachable; even his
men kept their distance unless they had urgent
business. He had little to say to them and even less
to say to his mother. He seemed to dislike her, in
fact, for all that he'd warned Maggie not to cause
her any sleepless nights.

"He keeps everyone at bay, doesn't he?" Maggie asked one afternoon when she was strolling
around the yard with Janet. The two women had
just watched Gabriel walk away from a man trying
to ask a question near the back porch.

Janet stared after him worriedly, her thin arms
folded across her chest. "He always has," she
said. "I don't think he's ever forgiven me for remarrying so soon after his father's death. The fact
that he hated my second husband made it worse.
He was...badly treated," she confessed, biting her
lower lip as the memories came back. "Stepfathers
are reluctant fathers at best. Ben liked Audrey and
Robin enough, of course; but they were just pretty
little girls and no threat to him. But Gabe was a
big boy, almost a teenager. He wound up fighting
for his very life. Ben shipped him off to a boarding

school, and I—'' she lowered her eyes ''—I was
caught between the two of them. I loved them both.
But I couldn't find the magic formula for making
them live together. It was that way until Ben died.
That was when Gabe was just out of the Marine
Corps.'' She shrugged. ''He came back and started
to pick up the pieces of his father's ranch—and
there were few, because my second husband was
much better at spending money than making it.
Gabe was bitter about it. He still is.''

''That doesn't seem enough to make a man as
cold as he is.'' Maggie probed gently.

Janet stared toward the tall man who was busy
saddling a horse out in the corral. ''You might as
well know it all,'' she said quietly. ''The year before Ben died, Gabriel found a young woman who
seemed to worship him. He brought her here, to
meet us, and she stayed for two weeks. During that
time, Ben was very attentive and managed to convince her that he was in control of all the finances
here and all the money.'' Shame-faced, Janet
closed her eyes. ''Ben ate up the attention. He was
dying, you see. He had cancer, and not long to live.
Gabe didn't know. But Ben was so flattered by the
girl's attention—he was just a man, after all. I
couldn't even blame him. But Gabe lost her, and
blamed Ben. And blamed me. Afterward, I tried to

tell him, to explain, but he wouldn't listen. He never would. To this day, he doesn't know. You see, Ben actually died of a heart attack. I didn't even tell the girls about the cancer."

"Oh, Janet, I'm sorry," Maggie said, touching the stooped shoulder lightly. "I'm so sorry. I shouldn't have asked."

"There, there, it was a long time ago," the older woman said through a stiff smile. "Gabe, needless to say, never got over it. Nor did he understand why I didn't leave Ben. After Ben died, Gabe came back from the service and stayed here, but the distance between us has been formidable. I think sometimes that he hates me. I've tried so hard, Maggie," she said softly. "I've tried so hard to show him that I care, that I was sorry, for so many things. I suppose playing Cupid was just another way of making restitution. But even that back-fired."

"People don't hold grudges forever," Maggie said gently.

"Don't they?" Janet replied, and her eyes were on her son, who was just mounting his horse. She shook her head and laughed. "I wonder."

"Have you told him about Becky?" Maggie asked suddenly. "Or why I'm really here?"

"Not yet," Janet confessed. "I've been waiting for the right time."

"He doesn't want me here," Maggie said. "And perhaps I should go back to San Antonio."

"No," Janet said firmly. "This is my home, too. I have a right to invite people here. He won't stop me. Or you."

"Janet, I'm so tired of fighting...."

"We'll keep out of his way," Janet assured her. "He'll be back at work in no time, you'll see, and then we'll have the place all to ourselves."

But she sounded no more certain than Maggie felt. And her apprehension intensified when Janet hesitantly asked Gabriel the next morning if he had a horse Maggie could ride.

"Please, I don't need to..." Maggie began quickly, noticing the dangerous look in Gabe's pale eyes.

"No, I don't have a spare horse," Gabe replied with a cold glare at Maggie. "I'm trying to get my calves branded, tagged and inoculated, and my herd out to summer pasture. Meanwhile, I'm being driven crazy by new hands who have to be led around like kids, I'm trying to keep supplies on hand with my ranch foreman off on sick leave, I'm a week behind on paperwork that my secretary can't do alone...I don't have time to be hounded by tourists!''

"Gabriel, there's no need to be rude," Janet chided.

He stood up. "She's your guest, not mine," he told his mother. "If you want her entertained, you entertain her."

And without another word, he left them sitting there, arrogantly lighting a cigarette as he went.

Maggie shivered as she stared after him half angrily. "A person could freeze to death just sitting near him," she muttered.

Janet shook her head and reached for her coffee. "I'm so sorry."

"You aren't responsible for his actions, and at least now I understand a little better than I did," Maggie told her with a smile. "It's all right. I'd like to stroll around a little, if you don't mind."

"I don't mind," Janet returned. "Just do stay out of his way, darling," she cautioned.

"You can count on that!" Maggie laughed.

She went out the back door, in fact, tugging on a yellow windbreaker over her beige blouse and jeans. It was still a little nippy, but she loved the coolness. She loved the outdoors, the land stretching lazily to the horizon, dotted with mesquite trees and prickly-pear cacti and wildflowers.

It was so different from her home in the middle of downtown San Antonio, so removed from urban traffic. Although the city was delightful and there was plenty to see and do, and colorful markets to visit, she was a country girl at heart. She loved the land with a passion she'd never given to anything else. Even now, with an enemy in residence, she could hardly contain her excitement at having so much land to explore, to savor.

She walked from the backyard down to the fence that stretched to the stables and stared over it at the few horses that were left. Most of them had gone out with the cowboys who were working the far-flung herds of cattle.

Her eyes were wistful as she stared at a huge black stallion. There wasn't a patch of white anywhere on him, and he looked majestic in the early-morning light. He tossed his mane and pranced around like a thoroughbred, as if he knew that he had an audience and was determined to give it its money's worth.

"Do you ride?"

The rough question startled her. She whirled, surprised to find Gabriel Coleman leaning against one of the large oak trees in the backyard, calmly smoking a cigarette while he stared at her.

She shifted a little. He looked bigger than ever

in that old long sleeved chambray shirt, and its color emphasized the lightness of his eyes under the wide brim of his hat. He was formidable in work clothes. So different from Dennis, who'd always seemed a bit prissy to Maggie.

"I...don't ride very well," she confessed.

He nodded toward the stallion. "I call him Crow. He was a thoroughbred with a bright future. But he killed a man and was going to be put down. I bought him and I ride him, but no one else does. There isn't a more dangerous animal on the place, so don't get any crazy ideas."

"I wouldn't dream of taking a horse without asking first," she said levelly. "Perhaps you're used to more impetuous women. I'm careful. I don't rush in without thinking."

His eyes narrowed at the insinuation, and he took a long draw from his cigarette. "Then why are you down here?" he asked coldly.

"Your mother invited me," she said.

"Why?"

"Why do you think?" she countered.

He smiled, and it wasn't friendly. He threw down the cigarette and moved toward her.

It was a deserted area. The house was hidden by a grove of oaks and pecan trees, and none of the men were around. Maggie, who'd had nightmares about physical intimacy since her marriage, began to back away until the cold bark of another oak tree halted her.

"Nervous?" he chided, and kept coming. "What of? I heard what Mother said the first night you were here. I know what you came for, Maggie. So why run away from it?"

She felt her body going rigid as he loomed over her, her eyes wide and green and frightened. "You don't understand…" she began.

"So you keep telling me," he said shortly. He rested his hands on either side of her head, blocking off all the exits, and he smelled of wind and fir trees and leather as he came even closer, favoring his right side a little where the arm was swollen.

"What is this?" she breathed.

"You're another consolation prize," he said with a mocking smile. "My mother thinks it's her fault that I'm such a lonely man. She brings me women by the gross. But I'm getting damned tired of being handed women on silver platters. When I marry, if I marry, I can choose my own bride. And I'll want something fresh and warm and sweet-smelling. A country girl—not a social butterfly who's been passed around like a plate of hors d'oeuvres."

Her lips opened to retaliate, but he pressed his thumb over them in a movement that startled her into silence. He'd always seemed like a cold, indifferent sort of man, but there was experience in the way he played with her mouth, and her surprise widened her eyes. How incredible, after all these years, to be this way with him, to see him as a man instead of an enemy; to feel the impact of his masculinity in a different way, a sensual way. Yes, he was experienced. His eyes told her so, and she wondered how she could have thought him cold when just the brush of his finger against her warm mouth was sending her mad.

"Yes, you like that, don't you, Maggie?" he whispered, his voice deep and slow and faintly contemptuous. "You didn't realize how sensitive your mouth was, did you? It can be teased and provoked into begging for a man's lips," he said softly, tracing the upper lip with the very edge of his thumb so that he could feel the moist underside and watch its sudden helpless trembling. "Like that," he murmured, increasing the pressure, seeing her face flush, her lips part involuntarily. Her body tautened, and he smiled because he knew why.

"No," she said on a sobbing breath, and even as she said it, she realized that he wasn't paying the least attention. He was powerfully made; she could feel the strength of him threatening her, the warmth that radiated from him with a leathery scent not at all unpleasant. Years ago, she'd dreamed of being touched, kissed, by him. She'd wanted him, and she'd known he was aware of it. But she'd also known, as he had, that such a thing was forbidden between them—because of her age. Her age had protected her...then. And she'd thought he was too cold to be tempted. Fool!

"Did you ever wonder?" he asked unexpectedly, tilting her chin as he bent. "Did you ever wonder how my mouth would feel moving on yours?"

Tears stung her eyes. It was fascinating that she could feel like this with him, that she could be hungry, physically, after what Dennis had done to her. She felt her own fingernails gripping the hard muscles of his upper arms, tugging gently. "Gabe," she whispered, giving in to the raging attraction.

"What did my mother offer you, Maggie?" he breathed against her mouth.

"Offer...me?" she whispered brokenly.

He moved closer, his legs trapping hers, his body demanding as his mouth hovered warmly over her lips. "She brought you down here for me.

She's given up bringing me career girls, so now she's dredging up old memories. She wants me to marry you.''

"Marry...you?" It was barely penetrating her hazy mind.

"Don't pretend," he said. His eyes were cold, not loverlike, as they met hers. "I heard you both plotting. Well, I'm not in the market for a wife, little Maggie," he said curtly. "But if you want to play around, I'm more than willing. You always did burn me up...."

Even as the last word faded in the air, his mouth came down on hers. But the tenderness she'd expected wasn't there. He was rough, as if the feel and taste of her had suddenly taken away his control. He made a sound, deep in his throat, and groaned as he pulled her too close and hurt his swollen arm. But he didn't let go. If anything, he was more ardent.

She felt his rough heartbeat and felt his strength with mute terror. "No!" she burst out. "Not...like this!" She tried to twist away from him.

He caught her hips with his, pressing them back against the rough bark of the tree. "What's the matter?" he taunted, lifting his mouth long enough to look down at her. "Does it take the promise of a wedding ring to get you in the mood?" His mocking voice sounded odd. Deep and slow and faintly strained.

Tears welled up behind her closed eyelids. Men weren't so different after all, she thought miserably. Sex was the only thing they wanted. Just sex. It was Dennis all over again, showing her how much stronger he was, forcing her to yield, taking what he wanted without the least thought of her comfort. She began to cry.

"Is it that bad?" he asked, his voice even and cold.

Her lips trembled. "I don't want...that," she whispered brokenly. "I don't want anyone. I just want...to be left alone."

He scowled. It seemed to get through to him finally that she was suffering him. Just that. Just suffering what he was doing to her. He could have sworn there was desire in her, at the beginning. But now she only looked afraid. She was as stiff as a rail, unyielding, cold.

With an economy of motion, he released her. She folded her arms across her breasts, trembling as she looked at him.

"Why the pretense?" he asked calculatingly. "Didn't my mother tell you why she invited you here?"

She swallowed, clutching herself tighter against

a sudden burst of wind. "Listen," she began, her voice shaking a little with reaction. "The only reason I came here was for some peace of mind. I have no inclination whatsoever to be your...your wife or your mistress or even your friend. It would suit me very well if I never saw you again!"

"Then why are you here?" he demanded coldly.

She smiled shakily. "I'm running away," she confessed. "Trying to find a way to keep my ex-husband from taking my little girl away from me. She's terrified of him, and so am I. He's remarried and has most of my money; and in a lawsuit for custody, I'll very likely lose. My daughter has a trust, you see. Dennis wants control of it."

He stared at her as if he'd been struck from behind. "Ex-husband?"

She nodded.

"Did he get the divorce, or did you?" he asked coldly.

"I did," she confessed.

"Poor man."

"He had enough women to console him, before and after," she returned, her voice empty and dull.

Her chin lifted as he looked down at her. "Are you that cold in bed?" he asked, half-angry and half-frustrated because he'd wanted her and he'd thought she'd wanted him back.

She stared at him unblinkingly, without speaking, until he had the grace to turn away, as if his own question had shocked him.

"Where is your daughter?"

She moved away from the tree slowly, careful to keep some distance between them. He lit another cigarette and leaned back against the tree she'd just vacated to study her curiously.

"She's in boarding school in San Antonio," she said. "Janet said that I could bring her here..."

"Hell!" he ground out.

"You don't need to worry about more people cluttering up your ranch," she said with what little pride she had left. "I'll be leaving as soon as the next bus is out, and Becky won't be coming up here, I promise." She shuddered as she looked at him, feeling the force of his masculinity even at a distance. She could still taste him on her mouth. "If there's no bus today, I'll hitchhike."

His pale eyes narrowed. "Afraid of me?" he taunted.

"Yes." And it was no lie.

He took a draw from the cigarette. "And what will you tell my mother about your abrupt departure?"

"I'll think of something."

"She'll be upset," he returned. "I've got enough trouble without having her in hysterics."

"I don't want—"

"How old is the girl?" he asked curiously.

"She's just six."

"What in hell is she doing in a boarding school, then?" he demanded. "What kind of mother are you?"

Tears threatened. "I have to work," she whispered. "I was afraid to leave her at home after school and on Saturdays, afraid Dennis might try to kidnap her. He threatened that. At the school, she's protected. He'd need a court order."

He sighed heavily. "What a hell of a life for a child that age."

He ought to know, she thought suddenly, and almost said it. But she had enough on her plate without deliberately antagonizing him.

"When does she get out of school?" he persisted.

"Next week. Next Friday."

He studied his cigarette for a long moment, then those cold eyes touched Maggie's face. "All right. Bring her here. But the two of you keep the hell out of my way, is that clear?"

"I don't want to stay here…"

"You'll stay," he returned shortly. "It's too late

now. I won't have Mother upset. Besides," he added, "at least you won't be running after me like her other 'guests.'"

"That's a fair statement."

He looked down his crooked nose at her, his hard lips smiling quietly. "Did I bruise you, honey?" he said in a tone that curled her toes. "I wanted to do that when you were sixteen. And you might as well not look so shocked. You wanted me to do it when you were sixteen."

She lowered her eyes. It was the truth. He'd been her very dream of perfection.

"Maggie."

She looked up again, her large green eyes sweeping his hard, dark face. "Yes?"

He shouldered away from the tree and caught her sudden withdrawal from him. His eyes narrowed thoughtfully.

"All right," he said with the first gentleness he'd shown since her arrival. "I won't touch you again. You'd better do something about your lip. I cut it when I kissed you."

She touched it with a finger and found a trace of blood there. She hadn't felt it. But she hadn't experienced so much emotional turmoil since her divorce.

He pulled out a handkerchief and offered it, noticing that she went to great lengths to avoid any contact with him when she took it and dabbed at her lip.

Her face felt hot, her knees weak. Odd that he should have such a profound effect on her. Perhaps it was just reaction.

"He hurt you, didn't he?" he asked suddenly, his gaze forceful. "He hurt you sexually."

She swallowed. "Yes."

"Then for God's sake, why have his child?" he demanded.

"I didn't have a lot of choice," she said, hiding her face.

He lit another cigarette, keeping his eyes on the match so that she wouldn't see them. He mumbled something harsh and forceful.

"It's all past history now," she said, and lifted her eyes. "I just want to pick up the pieces and raise my daughter. I don't want to trap you into marriage, honestly. I don't want anything to do with men, ever again. So I'll be glad to keep out of your way, if you'll stay out of mine."

He lifted his chin as he drew on the cigarette. "I don't bargain, honey."

"Don't call me that," she said coolly.

"I always used to; have you forgotten?" he asked, his voice oddly quiet. "I never tossed those words around like some men do, either. Too bad you didn't listen." Before she could pursue that, he was off on another subject. "Do you have a good lawyer?"

She shifted. "I suppose so."

"I'll make sure you do before the custody suit comes up."

"Listen here, Gabriel—"

"You were the only woman who ever called me that," he murmured, smoking his cigarette while he studied her. "I like it."

She tried again. "I don't want—"

"I'll fly you to get the little girl," he added, turning. "Let me know a day beforehand, so that I can arrange things."

"Will you listen!"

His eyebrows shot up. "To what?"

"I can arrange my own life...."

"You've made a hash of things, from what I've seen."

"I can do without your opinion!"

"Pity. You could use a few pointers. And before you jump to any conclusions," he added maddeningly, "I take back my offer to play around with you. In fact, I'll be generous and take back every damned thing I've said since you came here." He pursed his lips as he searched her puzzled eyes.

"You're like a virgin, aren't you? Afraid of sex, nervous of men…"

The blush got worse. Her fists clenched beside her body. "Are you quite through?"

"For now." He pulled the hat lower over his eyes. "Stay away from that stallion," he cautioned again.

She glared after him. Overbearing, domineering… She held the handkerchief to her lip again and caught a whiff of his spicy cologne. Why that scent should make her heart race was beyond her reasoning. Before she could wonder about her reaction, however, she turned furiously and went back into the house.

She spent a restless night worrying about whether or not she should just go back to San Antonio and make a stand there, without a vacation.

Her mind laughed at that. Some vacation, with Gabriel Coleman making vicious passes at her and threatening to take over her whole life. Of course, she had to admit that he'd gotten the whole situation wrong because of Janet's past matchmaking. And what he'd overheard that first night could have sounded like a plan to trap him at the altar.

She flushed, remembering what she'd confessed about having had a crush on him. Had he heard that, too? It would have been hard to miss, though, because at sixteen her eyes had followed him everywhere. The girls had even teased her about being so taken with him, and she didn't doubt that they'd told him, too.

He'd always been more man than the average woman could handle. Something in her had always been, and still was, a little afraid of him. But underneath the cold, hard exterior, there seemed to be a surprisingly gentle man. She'd had a glimpse of that, and she'd warmed to it helplessly. Gentleness was the one thing she'd never had from Dennis, who took and gave nothing in return. Looking back, she could see his deviousness with clear eyes. But at eighteen she'd been flattered by his charming attentions and been on fire to marry and have children.

How sad, she thought as she closed her eyes, that so often what people wanted the most was the last thing that could make them happy. What was the old saying about being careful what you wished for because you might get it? She wished she'd been a little more clearheaded at eighteen. Perhaps if her parents hadn't moved to Austin, perhaps if Gabriel had really been interested in her, if he'd come courting…

She went to sleep and dreamed about that. And woke up warm all over. It seemed the scars weren't quite as deep as she'd thought—or else how could she have that kind of dream about Gabriel?

Chapter Four

Maggie managed to keep Janet from finding out about her disastrous confrontation with Gabe. As for him, his attitude toward her was a little less hostile. He made no more passes at her, and he stopped baiting her. But there was no drastic change in his manner. He was much as he had been before he'd learned the truth. If he felt anything at all except irritation, he hid it well. Perhaps he'd learned over the years to keep his deepest emotions hidden, Maggie thought. Heaven knew he'd had reason to.

His arm was still giving him brief twinges of pain—that was obvious—but a few days later he climbed on a horse despite the discomfort and rode out to help his men. He was kept busy, disability notwithstanding, with the separate herds of cattle, as he and his men worked increasingly long hours. Janet seemed relieved, although she didn't say anything.

The following Thursday night, Maggie was forced to wait up for Gabe. He'd promised to fly down to get Becky the next day. And it was either that or ask Janet to face the long drive into San Antonio on her behalf. Maggie laughed mirthlessly, thinking about the past, when she could easily have chartered a plane to take her. Thanks to Dennis and his spendthrift ways, that was no longer an option. If only she'd had more backbone in the beginning! If only she hadn't knuckled under! But she'd made her own bed by refusing to take action, and now she was paying for it horribly.

When Janet started upstairs about nine o'clock, Gabe still hadn't come home. Maggie was reading a book on the sofa, curled up under a lap blanket in jeans and a multicolored pullover blouse.

"Are you going to stay up for a while?" Janet asked casually.

"I'm waiting for him," Maggie said, knowing that the older woman would understand she meant Gabe. "He said he'd fly me down to get Becky tomorrow if I'd remind him. I have to see if he meant it."

"My son never says things he doesn't mean," Janet said, and actually seemed to relax. "I didn't know you'd told him about Becky, although I had a few suspicions. He's stopped cutting at you so much."

"Not noticeably." Maggie sighed. "Yes, I told him. I mentioned getting a bus, and he wouldn't hear of it. But I don't know how he'll manage time."

"Stand back and watch." Janet grinned. "Oh, my dear, I'm so glad he offered. I wouldn't have minded driving down with you...."

"But it's a tiring trip," she reminded the older woman. "It was kind of him to offer."

"I think he's curious about your daughter," Janet said suddenly. "He's not an easy man to get along with, but he loves children. It's something of a tragedy that he never married, you know. He would have been a good father."

That was surprising. He didn't seem the kind of man who would warm to a child, but Maggie knew she was no judge of men—not after the brutal mistake she'd made.

Long after Janet had gone upstairs, Maggie thought over what she'd said about her taciturn son. He was such an enigma. He wasn't handsome; in fact, he was rather plain. And although his mother seemed to think he was unable to attract women, Maggie knew he wasn't an inexperienced man. He'd known exactly what he was doing when he'd made that pass at her in the backyard. If it hadn't been for her unfortunate marriage, it might have been difficult not to respond to his ardor. His mouth had been hard and warm and very, very expert, and something deep inside her had reacted wildly to the taste of him, although she'd kept him from knowing it.

The sound of the front door opening disturbed her thoughts. She let the book lie open in her lap and looked into the hall. The glimpse she got of the real Gabriel Coleman in that instant was fascinating.

He didn't know anyone was around, and all the mocking arrogance was gone. He was quiet and solemn, and he looked every year of his age. Dust covered him from his blue check shirt to his stained jeans and wet boots. His black hair was disheveled and damp as well, and his face was heavily lined. He tossed his hat onto the hall table and dropped the wide leather chaps he'd just discarded onto the floor. He stretched, his hard muscles shuddering a little with the strain they'd been under. Then, as he looked toward the living room and saw Maggie watching him, all the hardness returned to his face, and to his pale, penetrating eyes.

"Couldn't you sleep?" he asked with a mocking smile. "If you're looking for the obvious remedy, sorry, I'm too tired to oblige."

As she searched his face quietly, it suddenly dawned on her that he didn't really mean half the cutting things he said. They seemed to be a kind of camouflage to keep women from getting close to him, from looking beneath the savage surface. And at that realization, all the hot words poised on the tip of her tongue faded away, forgotten.

"You said you'd fly me down to San Antonio to get Becky tomorrow," she said gently. "I hate to remind you; you look so tired."

His face froze, as if the unexpected compassion had off-balanced him. "I remember."

She got to her feet. Bare feet, because she hated shoes, and hers were under a chair somewhere. "I don't know if you have time now, with things so hectic here," she continued, facing him beside the couch. "I need to know, so that I can make other arrangements...."

He had just noticed her bare feet, and it seemed

as if he were having problems keeping back a grin. "Lost your shoes, Cinderella?"

Her bare toes wiggled. "I hate shoes," she muttered. "I even got Becky into the habit around the house, and when she went back to school, she got kept in at recess for it."

"Does she like it at that school?" he asked unexpectedly.

"I suppose so." Maggie hesitated. "She doesn't talk about it. She's a very shy child." She frowned. "She's so easily upset. Perhaps it would be better if I just went home now."

He cocked an eyebrow and slowly lit a cigarette, without once moving his eyes from her face. "What are you afraid of? That I'll upset her? You might be surprised at the way she reacts to my temper, city girl. Most people around here aren't that intimidated by it."

"Of course not," she agreed innocently. "That's why your men hide in the bushes every morning until you're out of sight."

That did produce a smile, of sorts. "Kids see more than adults," he returned mysteriously. "I'll have to get things organized before I can leave. We'll get away about nine."

"You're sure you don't mind?" she persisted.

"I don't put myself out for anyone unless it suits me," he said curtly.

"Then, thank you. I'll be ready."

She started past him, only to find his strong hand on her upper arm, halting her beside him.

"How old are you now?" he asked, his eyes all too close, too searching. It didn't help that her gaze dropped to his hard mouth and remembered vividly its exciting touch.

"I—I'm twenty-five," she stammered.

He studied her quietly. "I'm thirty-eight."

"Yes, I know."

His eyes probed hers in a silence that began to simmer, until the world narrowed to the space they occupied. He turned, just a little, and the cigarette went careening into a large ashtray so that both lean hands could hold her there.

She flinched, and he shook his head.

"No," he said softly. Softly! It was the first time she'd heard that slow, tender note in his deep voice. "I won't be rough with you. Not ever again."

Her body seemed to vibrate as she looked up at him uncomprehendingly.

"I've never deliberately hurt a woman before," he said slowly. "It's just that I've had so damned many prospective brides flung at my head...." His hands slid up her arms, over her shoulders, to cup her face. "I don't like having you flinch from me, Margaret," he whispered, bending. "So I'm going to show you what it should have been like."

"But I don't…" she whispered unsteadily.

He poised there, his pale eyes narrow and flashing as they met hers. "Say my name," he breathed roughly.

"Gabe…"

As the syllable faded, he took it into his mouth. Her eyelids trembled and then closed. It was nothing like before. His lips were hard and warm but softly probing this time, brushing, lifting, savoring in a sweet tasting that was beyond her experience of men.

"That's it," he whispered against her slowly parting lips. "That's right, let me have your mouth. I won't hurt it this time."

A tiny, soundless sob broke as he parted her lips tenderly and fit his own to them with a warm, maddening pressure that made her body ache with new and unexpected sensations.

Her hands opened over his shirt, feeling muscle and the soft prickliness of hair underneath their cool palms. His heart was beating slowly, regularly, until her nails contracted, and then his chest began to rise and fall quickly.

His lean fingers stroked gently through her hair, tilting her head back, his mouth insistent as it probed hers in a rhythm that surprised a moan from her.

She felt one of his hands spread against her cheek, and while his mouth was tormenting hers, his thumb rubbed across her lips, sensitizing them, grazing them against her teeth. She made another sound, one she didn't even recognize, and her nails bit into his chest.

"Gabriel." Was that whimper coming from her lips? She was reaching up without realizing it, trying to get closer, to make him kiss her more ardently, more completely.

He obliged her with lazy indulgence, forcing her head back against his shoulder with the hungry but controlled pressure of his mouth opening on hers. She felt his tongue teasing her lips, tasting their inner softness, and her body seemed to throb where it sought his.

One lean hand moved then, easing down over her shoulder to the soft blouse, finding only softer woman beneath it, and no bra—finding a hard peak that aroused him beyond bearing. His hand slid farther down, over her narrow waist, the curve of her hip, and around to the base of her spine. He drew her hips in slowly until they merged with his, and he gloried in her sudden trembling as she felt the fierce arousal of his body.

"No," she pleaded, trying feebly to turn her head. "Oh, you mustn't!"

He didn't insist. His hand slid back up to her face, brushing away the damp hair, tilting her chin so that he could look into her misty, dazed eyes above a mouth that was parted and softly swollen from his kisses.

"Was he ever able to make you want him?" he whispered softly.

"No...oh, not ever like this," she sobbed, hating her inability to lie to him.

His fingers caressed her face gently. "There's nothing to be embarrassed about," he said, his voice deep and slow as he watched her. "You're pretty much a novice, despite your marriage. An experienced man knows how to make himself acceptable to a woman."

She was still trying to get her breath back, and his body against hers was warm and hard and welcome. "You've...had women," she whispered, searching the eyes that weren't so hard after all.

He nodded. He looked down at her yielding body, then back up at her parted lips. "And with very little effort, I could have you," he said quietly. "But that isn't what I want. This was a nonverbal apology, nothing more. I don't need the practice.''

Before she could react to that, he eased her away, steadying her. "Want something to drink?" he asked then, as casually as if they'd just met.

"A...a brandy.''

"Sit down. I'll get it.''

She curled up in an armchair, her heart beating wildly, her eyes like green saucers in a face flushed with unexpected pleasure.

He dashed brandy into two snifters, passed her one, and perched on the arm of her chair while she sipped at it with jerky motions.

"I...should go home,'' she burst out, thinking out loud.

"Why?'' he asked. "I won't seduce you.'' He tilted her chin up and looked into her eyes, noting her scarlet blush, her quickened breathing. "More than likely, I'd get you pregnant,'' he said with more amusement than irritation.

"No, you wouldn't,'' she replied, her voice still a trifle unsteady. "I'm on the pill. I had a slight female dysfunction, and the doctor put me on it to regulate me. So I'm not...vulnerable that way.''

His eyebrows arched and he smiled slowly. "Then suppose you come up to bed with me.''

"I don't believe in that kind of thing," she said quietly.

"No wedding ring, no sex?" he taunted. "How old-fashioned of you, Miss Margaret."

"Anyway," she countered, staring at her drink, "sex isn't all that fabulous for women."

"Think so?" Again he tilted her chin to force her eyes up to his. "I've had women claw my back raw, and it wasn't because I was hurting them."

She flushed to the roots of her hair, barely able to breathe at all.

"I could make you claw me, too," he breathed at her lips. "I could make you writhe like a wild thing under my body and scream with the need to have me."

"You shouldn't…say things like that," she said brokenly.

"You're more a virgin than a divorced woman with a child," he returned, searching her eyes. "Was there any other man?"

"No," she whispered. "Only…him."

"In the ways that count, you're untouched," he murmured. "A walking green-eyed challenge. Too bad, Margaret, that we didn't ignore the obstacles all those years ago and take what we really wanted from each other. I might have broken your young heart, but I'd have made you whole in every other way. We have an unusually potent chemical reaction to each other. We always did.''

She knew that, but it didn't make her feel particularly good to have it reduced to technical terms.

He threw down the rest of his brandy and stood up, his back to her. "You'd better get some rest, honey. We'll have a long trip ahead of us."

"Yes. Of course." She finished her own brandy, put the snifter down and stood up.

He turned, towering over her. "He cowed you, didn't he?" he asked unexpectedly, his eyes narrow, calculating. "You're nothing like the woman I remember. All that sweet wildness I used to watch in you is gone."

"I got tired of being slapped down," she replied. "He got his revenge...in bed."

"Oh, God," he breathed roughly.

She looked up, searching his eyes. "You'd never be cruel that way," she said, knowing it. "You might cut a woman with words, but you'd never be physically cruel. Even that day, in the backyard, you didn't really hurt me."

"Didn't I?" he said curtly. "I cut your mouth."

It seemed to bother him that he had. She put a finger to his lower lip, where her own teeth had bitten into it in her passion minutes before. He stiffened at the light contact.

"I cut yours," she whispered.

His jaw clenched and his breathing was audible. "In passion," he whispered back. "Not in anger."

She withdrew her hand with a small laugh. "I never suspected that I was capable of passion."

She turned away, oblivious to the blinding hunger in the pale eyes of the man behind her. "Good night— Oh!"

He'd pulled her around. "Say my name, saucy girl," he whispered, teasing her. "Come on."

"I won't," she said, feeling a rising new excitement.

His lip tugged up. "Say it," he challenged, pulling her body against his, "or I'll kiss you blind."

He could have, too. She drew in a jerky breath. "Gabriel," she said.

He let her go with a faint smile. "Good night." And he walked away without another word.

Enigma, she thought confusedly. Enigma. She'd never known anyone like him. And her body was sending out smoke signals, begging for him. She'd never expected complications like this. And now she didn't know what to do.

At precisely nine o'clock the next morning, when Maggie came downstairs dressed in a neat gray suit, Gabe was waiting for her at the front door. He was wearing gray, too, a vested suit that made him look debonair, sophisticated, almost handsome—and every inch a very male man. He smelled of spicy cologne and soap, and Maggie wondered why she couldn't seem to stop staring at him. She gripped her purse as Janet came out to say goodbye.

"I'd go with you," she told Maggie, "but it's less crowded this way. Have a safe trip."

"I'll take care of her," Gabe said carelessly. He spared his mother a glance and walked off without even a smile.

Maggie didn't say a lot on the way to the airstrip. She was curious about him, in so many ways. She wanted to ask questions, to learn new things. And that was dangerous.

"Nervous?" Gabe asked after a minute, glancing at her wickedly as he lifted his cigarette to his lips.

"Not really. I'm not afraid of flying," she murmured evasively.

"And that wasn't what I meant, either." He pulled off the main ranch road onto a dirt track with deep ruts that led toward the airstrip and the big hangar where he kept his twin-engine planes. He had two, he explained: one for work, for herding cattle; the other for business trips.

"Don't you ever fly for pleasure?" she asked.

Gabe glanced at her. "I have women for pleasure, when I can't stand the ache any longer. That's about the extent of my recreational activities these days."

She stared out the window, embarrassed despite her age and experience. "You're very blunt."

"I don't pull my punches—about anything," he replied. "I believe in total honesty. I've never yet found a woman who did."

"Your mother told me that you…" She stopped when she realized what she was betraying.

His icy-blue eyes cut at her. "Did she tell you all of it, or aren't you that privileged?" he asked with bitter sarcasm.

"I'm sorry. It's none of my business. I shouldn't have said anything."

He took a deep draw from the ever-present cigarette and drove faster. "My God, is nothing sacred these days?"

"She thought it might help me to understand things a little better," Maggie replied quietly.

"Did it?" he asked cuttingly.

She met his brief glance. "Yes. It explained everything."

He searched her eyes quickly and then turned back to the road, slowing as they approached the airstrip. "I hated him," he said. "Even before that happened. I saw through him a hell of a long time before she did. And in spite of it, she wouldn't leave him.''

"Love imprisons people, so I've heard," she said.

"Didn't you love your husband?" Gabe asked, his smile mocking.

"I thought I did," she replied. "He was charming. Utterly charming. I was shy in those days, and overwhelmed that such a handsome man would be interested in me. I was an heiress, you know. Filthy rich.''

"Yes. I remember," he said bitterly. He stared at the airplane in the distance, watching a mechanic go over the large red-and-white Piper Navajo. "Our place had fallen on hard times when you were a teenager."

"I didn't know." She stared at her lap. "Dennis had fallen on hard times, too. I was eighteen," she said. "Green as grass and infatuated, and every time he kissed me, I was on fire. And then we got married." She shuddered. "My God, for all my reading, I never realized the things men would expect of women in bed!"

He scowled. "What, exactly, did he want of you?"

Maggie flushed. "I can't tell you."

"I think I can guess, all the same," he said, his eyes narrowing.

She stared at her crossed hands. Amazing how easy it was to talk to him about such intimate things. "When I froze, he accused me of being frigid. From then on, it got worse. I didn't even mind that much when he started seeing other women. It was almost a relief, except that it stung my pride. I'd planned to leave him. And then I discovered that I was pregnant."

"You stuck it out for a long time," he observed.

"My mother was still alive then," she replied. "She'd told me what to do all my life; I was afraid to go against her. She said that divorce was an unspeakable scandal, that nobody in her family had ever been divorced. So I didn't disgrace her. After she died, it didn't seem to matter anymore. The money was gone; there were no social peers to be scandalized by what I did."

"You said that your daughter was afraid of him," he reminded her.

"Becky's easily hurt," she said. "He terrifies her. He drinks, you see." She sighed. "The last time he had a visiting session with her, she did something that upset him. He left some marks on her. She's been afraid of him ever since."

Gabe said something under his breath that embarrassed her and braked to a halt beside the airstrip tarmac. "Is he suing for sole custody?" he asked, turning to look at her.

"Yes."

"We'll see your attorney while we're in San Antonio." He opened the car door. "And if he doesn't suit me, you'll use mine."

"Now, wait a minute," Maggie began as he came around to open her door.

"You wait a minute," he countered, helping her out. He held her just in front of him, towering over her slender height. "If that child is on my property, she's my responsibility. So are you, for that matter. And until you leave, I'll take care of you, whether you like it or not!"

"You...you...Texas bulldozer!" she accused, eyes flashing as they hadn't since her childhood.

"Go ahead, argue with me," he responded, smiling slightly. "Make a fuss. And when I've had enough, guess how I'll deal with you?"

She has a good idea, but she wasn't backing down. "That's—that's male chauvinism," she sputtered.

"I'm a man, all right," he replied without the least bit of self-reproach. "Come on, honey. Make a fuss."

He looked as if he'd really enjoy that, and Maggie remembered how it had been in the backyard that day, when he'd backed her against the oak tree and taken what he'd wanted. Her face colored.

His blue eyes sparkled with pure enjoyment. "That's exactly what I'd do, you little prude. Only this time, I'd go further than a few kisses, and it wouldn't be in anger or bad temper. I'd wear you down and lay you down, and when I got through, you'd ache for me the rest of your life."

"Conceited jackass," she enunciated clearly.

He laughed softly. "Am I? Apparently, Miss Maggie, you've forgotten how you react to me. You always did get flustered and nervous when I came too close, even at sixteen." His pale-blue eyes narrowed as they traveled down her slender body, making her tingle with the frank appraisal. "You always were a beauty, to me. Especially in a bathing suit, with that long black hair down to your waist.... Why did you cut it?" he asked unexpectedly.

She sighed. "I thought it looked too girlish for a woman my age," she told him, then smiled. "And it was hot in the summer."

"Would it shock you to know that I used to dream about wrapping it around my wrist?" Gabe asked, his voice gentle. "And pillowing you on it, while I laid you down on one of those loungers that used to sit by the pool?''

Again Maggie colored, but she didn't look away. She seemed to blush all the time around him! ''Did you really?'' she asked.

He nodded. ''It got to be more than disturbing, especially considering the age difference. I'll be blunt, Maggie, I was glad when you stopped coming here to see the girls. You caused me some sleepless nights.''

''You heard what I said to Janet, didn't you?'' she asked suddenly. ''About having a crush on you?''

''Yes. But I knew already.'' His eyes narrowed, glittering. ''That was what worried me so much. Your eyes were sultry and just faintly hungry when you looked at me. I knew I could do anything I wanted to you, and you'd let me. The thought tormented me.''

She'd thought about that, too; about having him kiss her and make love to her. Her heart went wild in her chest. She wondered suddenly and startlingly what it would feel like to make love with him.

''We'd better get going,'' he said, missing the shock in her eyes. ''Come on.''

He held out his hand and stood there until she

took it, refusing to budge an inch. She yielded because she knew him so well. He'd die before he gave in, once he got his mind set on something. She even admired it, that stubborn streak of his. The feel of his strong hand around hers was intoxicating. She let him hold it while she wondered how she was going to keep him from taking her over, lock, stock and daughter. Odd, she thought as they approached the plane, how delicious it was to be close to him....

Then they were on their way, and she stopped thinking about it.

Chapter Five

The exclusive boarding school where Becky stayed was frantic with activity. Gabe looked around him curiously as little girls rushed down the hall outside the office where he and Maggie waited for Becky.

"Margaret, thank goodness!" Mrs. Hayes burst out as she joined them, closing her office door gingerly behind her. "I didn't know what to do. He's been here for thirty minutes. I knew you were coming since you called this morning...."

"Dennis is here?" she gasped. "Oh, Mrs. Hayes, you didn't let him have Becky?"

"Of course not, dear. He's in my office...."

Gabe moved her gently aside and made a beeline

for the office, his long strides eating up the distance. Maggie, sensing disaster, rushed after him and Mrs. Hayes just stared, biting her lip.

Gabe thrust open the door and a shorter, younger, fair-haired man jerked around in surprise, his eyes wide and shocked as he stared at the formidable Westerner.

"Maggie, darling..." Dennis laughed nervously, staring past the tall man to a less intimidating presence. "I didn't expect you so early. I was just going to drive Becky over to your house for you."

"Like hell you were," Gabe said coldly. "But I can save you the trouble. I'm taking Maggie and the child home with me."

Dennis glared at the bigger man. "Who are you?"

"Gabriel Coleman."

Dennis straightened, finding unexpected new ammunition in the curt response. Gabriel Coleman... He remembered everything he'd heard about the man. And now, seeing him, it wasn't hard to believe it was all true. So this was the Texas rancher Maggie's father had wanted her to marry. Maggie probably didn't know that, but Dennis did. Her father had used it like a nagging prod every time they'd met socially. He smiled. "So, that's how it is. Living with your old lover, are you? Janice and I got married Monday, so I've really got the edge on you now, haven't I?" he added. "It won't look good in court when everyone sees what an unfit mother you are."

"You can't take her," Maggie cried. "You can't! All you want is the money!"

"She's my child," Dennis replied arrogantly. "And I've got a lot more right to her, married, than you do single and living with your…lover," he added, with a cold glare at Gabriel. "You couldn't wait, could you? Well, he'll find you as frigid as I—"

He stopped in midsentence as Gabe, imperturbably unruffled by the outburst, lifted him half off the floor by the collar and escorted him out of the office and down the hall.

"By God, that's enough," Gabe was muttering to Dennis. "How she could marry something like you in the first place is beyond me."

Becky came into the office before Gabe returned and ran into her mother's outstretched arms.

"Oh, Mama," Becky wailed. "Michelle said Daddy was here." She drew away, green eyes wide and frightened. "I don't have to go with him, do I?"

"No, darling," Maggie said softly, hoping, praying that it would be the truth after the custody battle was over. She knelt, smiling at the young girl, brushing back the long strands of hair from the pale little face. "No, you don't have to go with him."

Becky looked past her mother and her face froze. She frowned a little. "Who are you?" she asked curiously.

"Gabriel Coleman," he said, looking down at her with narrowed eyes.

Becky's face lit up. "You're Aunt Janet's Gabe, aren't you?" the little girl asked, moving toward the tall man. She looked up at him with open fascination. "Aunt Janet says that you have a ranch and horses and cows and lots of cowboys, just like in the movies! Do you shoot Indians?"

Incredibly, the hard face relaxed into a genuine smile, the first one Maggie had seen yet. He went down on one knee so that he could see Becky better. "No, I don't shoot Indians," he said, amused. "But I have a couple of Commanche men who work for me."

Becky's face brightened. "Do they scalp people?"

He looked up at Maggie. "I'd love to hear the bedtime stories you tell this child."

Maggie flushed. "Well, actually, it's the movies…"

"You'd better come home with me, Becky," he said seriously, "and you can see what ranching is like for yourself."

Becky hesitated. There was fear in her eyes—the same fear Gabe had seen in her mother—and his face hardened visibly.

"Your mother will be there, too," he said softly. "And I swear, honey, nobody will hurt you as long as I'm around."

Becky's wan little face managed a wobbly smile. "Then I guess it'll be okay."

He nodded. "Are you ready?" he asked, standing.

"Yes, sir. I have my suitcase right over there."

Gabe picked it up, glancing at Maggie over the child's head. There was an expression in his eyes that defied description.

Becky was delighted with the ranch. She'd been quiet all the way back, except to exclaim at the private plane and the fact that Gabe could actually fly it. But when she got her first look at the ranch, her breath sighed out in a rush.

"Oh, isn't it just beautiful, Mama?" she asked Maggie, all eyes and laughter. "Isn't it just beautiful? Look at all the room! And cows and horses…!"

Gabe chuckled softly, smoking his cigarette without comment.

"Can I ride a horse? Oh, can I?" Becky begged.

"No," Maggie said.

"Yes," Gabe countered immediately, his eyes challenging Maggie. "She's old enough. I was four when my dad put me on my first horse. I won't let her get hurt," he added gently when she still hesitated.

Maggie bit her lip. She'd need a lot more sustenance than the rushed breakfast she'd had to take on Gabriel Coleman in that mood. But it was going to be a fight all the way; of that she was sure.

Janet was delighted to see the child and made a big fuss over her. Even the housekeeper began immediately to spoil her. She was taken off into the kitchen and then upstairs to see her very own room. Everyone was enthusiastic except Maggie, who'd had a glimpse of hell at the boarding school.

Dennis had almost succeeded in spiriting the child away, and possession was still nine-tenths of the law. If she'd been a little later, or if Gabe hadn't been with her... She shuddered to think of the consequences.

And now Dennis thought she had a lover. He was going to use Gabe, of all people, against her. How would she prove it was a lie? It might be just the lever Dennis needed to get possession of Becky, and what a hell of a life she'd have with him. If it came to that, Maggie might be forced to take the child and run. She glanced at Gabe, at the sheer magnificence of him. Her mother and father had always adored him. Perhaps they'd said something to Dennis in the early days of their marriage, something that had made him suspicious. Dennis had an active imagination, and he was good at twisting the truth to suit himself. She dreaded the thought of having him create a scandal that would involve Janet as well as Gabe.

Gabe was watching her closely over dinner. After Becky was tucked up in bed and Janet had gone upstairs, he waylaid Maggie and dragged her off into his study.

"Let's talk," he said curtly, motioning her into an armchair.

She refused his offer of brandy and sat with her hands folded primly in her lap. "What about?" she asked hesitantly.

"About that little girl upstairs," he returned, dropping into an armchair across from her. "And why she's terrified of men. What did that son of a rattlesnake do to her?"

"Dennis in a temper can do that even to big people," Maggie said miserably. She studied the hard lines of his face. "Oddly enough, I'm not afraid of your temper. Not anymore," she added with a faint smile. "I used to be. I'll never forget the day you beat up that cowboy at the grocery store in town."

His eyes darkened, narrowed. "He touched you," he said curtly, as if that explained everything. "He put his hands on you. I could have broken his neck."

She stared at him, curiously. "I wondered," she murmured, her voice barely carrying. "I always wondered if it was because of that."

He shifted in the chair, bringing the brandy to his lips to break the spell. "You didn't know anything about men. I wasn't going to let one of my hands back you into a corner."

She studied his lean, beautifully masculine hands, wrapped around the brandy snifter. "You always were like a bulldozer."

"When I wanted something," he agreed. He studied her over the rim of the snifter. "I wanted you. But you were sixteen."

She colored softly and stared into his eyes. "You never did anything about it."

"I told you why. You were sixteen." He swished the amber liquid around, watching the patterns it made in the glass. "I might have gotten around to it, if you hadn't gone off to boarding school.'' He smiled slowly. ''It would have been the last straw, trying to take you out with all those giggling girls watching.''

Her lips trembled into a smile. ''Really? Would you have?''

''I suppose I'd have come to it eventually,'' he said enigmatically, shrugging his wide shoulders. ''You were a pretty kid. You still are, haunted eyes and all.'' He searched those eyes, watching the shadows in them. ''You aren't afraid of me physically.''

''Yes, I know.'' She twisted a strand of her short hair uneasily and watched him. He'd taken off his jacket and vest and unfastened the top buttons of his white shirt. Dark skin and darker hair were visible in the deep V, and she felt a thrill of excitement at the memory of being held against his long, hard body.

He laughed, his voice deep in the stillness. ''Don't start getting nervous. I'm not going to pounce on you. I hope I have more finesse than that, especially after what you've been through.''

She studied her hands. ''I don't suppose anything frightens you. But I'm not physically strong, and I've had years of abuse, mental and physical.

I carry my scars where they don't show, but they're very deep. So are Becky's.''

He leaned back in the armchair, and for once he wasn't smoking like a furnace.

"Becky's young. Hers will heal. But yours won't. Not without help.'' He watched her with narrowed eyes, his dark head like ebony in the overhead light.

"Are you offering me the cure?'' she asked, feeling bitter. "A little sexual therapy?''

He lifted an eyebrow. "I'm not that damned unselfish,'' he replied quietly. "And I don't need therapy. No, honey,'' he added, leaning forward to pin her with his pale eyes. "If I made love to you, it wouldn't be a cure; but it might be an addiction.''

Heat seemed to well up inside her. She averted her eyes to the carpeted floor. Just to think of having him touch her that way made her heart run wild. Magic, when intimacy had been such a dark thing in her life.

"Shy little girl,'' he said with tender amusement. "Look at me, coward.''

She lifted her face, hating its reddened color and vulnerability. "Stop making fun of me.''

"Is that what I'm doing?'' he asked. "I thought I was flirting.''

She really colored then and started to get to her feet. He rose at the same time, catching her arm gently in his free hand, to hold her just in front of him. He towered over her, all steely strength and masculine dominance, smelling of tangy cologne and soap.

"I haven't spent much time around women in the past few years," he said, his voice deep and slow in the stillness. "I'm rusty at social skills, so you'll have to get used to a little embarrassment now and then. All you have to remember is that I'm no pretty boy with a line a mile long. I'm a country man with old-fashioned ideas and I'll never hurt you. Physically or emotionally."

"Are you trying to tell me that you won't seduce me if I smile at you?" she asked, testing emotions she hadn't used in over six years as she looked up at him.

He didn't move. He seemed to be holding his breath. In fact, he was. The softness in those green eyes held him spellbound. He hadn't realized just how vulnerable he was.

"That's about the size of it. You don't trust men, do you?" He touched her face with hesitant fingers. "I suppose we're alike in being wary. I thought I was in love a few times, but I got burned badly once. I guess I've forgotten how to trust women in the years since.''

He sounded just faintly vulnerable, and something inside her stirred like a budding flower. She searched his face. "Damaged people," she whispered.

He understood immediately, his nod more eloquent than speech. He brushed the back of his finger over her soft mouth. "Come here and kiss me."

He bent as he spoke, and without the slightest hesitation she rose on tiptoe and kissed him. It was the first move she'd ever made of her own free will toward a man. He made everything so natural, so easy. She was sixteen again, feeling her first passion for a man. And there was Gabe, tough and hard and filling her world, her life.

"Gabe," she whispered brokenly, holding him gently as she pressed her warm, soft mouth against his and flew up into the sun with the powerful response he gave her.

She felt his hand at the back of her head, pressing her lips hard against his, and then she was free and he'd moved away, turned away, so that she couldn't see the effect she'd had on him. But when he put the brandy snifter down to light a cigarette, she noticed his hand wasn't quite steady.

"You're just dynamite," she said dazedly.

He turned, his eyes shocked, delighted. He smiled at her. "Hell, so are you."

It was a real smile, not a smirk or sarcasm. He lit the cigarette but his eyes held hers, searched them slowly. "Are you going to be that honest with me from now on?" he asked. "Because I'll have to warn you, it's dangerous."

"Telling the truth?"

"Telling me the truth about what you feel when I touch you," he told her. "My God, I've got a low boiling point with you, Maggie," he added softly, fervently. "I never dreamed it would be like that."

"Neither did I," she said, her voice soft, colored with what she was feeling so unexpectedly. "I…used to…" She stopped, horrified at what she was about to reveal.

"Used to what?" he coaxed, moving closer. "Used to what, honey?" he repeated, touching her lips gently.

"I used to daydream about you," she murmured, lowering her eyes to his hard chest. "About kissing you."

"You weren't the only one." He tilted up her chin. "The reality is pretty devastating. I gather it wasn't like that with your ex-husband?"

She shook her head. "I never really wanted him physically," she said. "I suppose he knew.... Do men know?" she asked, lifting plaintive eyes.

He nodded slowly. "I would, anyway," he said. "It's hard to fake."

"He couldn't make me want him. That made it worse. He had so many women, and I tried not to mind, but after a while, I felt like a Medusa."

"Why did you marry him?" he asked.

She shrugged. "He was a lot of fun. He'd take me places and give me things." She smiled sadly. "I'd never had a man pay me any attention. Not like that. I was a pushover."

"I could have," he said half under his breath, and the look in his eyes disturbed her. "If you hadn't been so young, honey..."

"You were almost thirty," she remembered, searching his hard face. "Already a grown man. You fascinated me."

"I know." There was a world of emotion in those two words. He brushed back the hair from her temple, his fingers warm and hard and strong. "And frightened you. It was because of me that you stopped coming here to see the girls, wasn't it?"

"Yes," she confessed softly, smiling. "I knew I couldn't hide what I was feeling. I was afraid you'd see it and make fun of me or be embarrassed.''

"I wouldn't have done either," he told her, his voice gentle. "I'm not sure how I would have handled it, but I'd have managed without hurting your pride too much." He pursed his lips musingly. "I lost track of you after the girls left school. I always meant to look you up again, but your family moved to Austin.''

"It's just as well," she said. "You'd have wanted more than I could give.''

He smoothed her hair. "No, I wouldn't have," he said firmly. "I'd have respected your innocence. I wouldn't have asked you to give it to me without a commitment." His chest rose and fell slowly. "Maggie, are you going to be able to handle a physical relationship again?''

She felt her body relaxing against his, felt her helpless reaction to his strength. Her fingers played with a button on his shirt, and she bit her lower lip, succumbing to old memories and new hungers all at once.

"I don't know," she said.

He nuzzled her cheek with his. "Shall we find out?''

Her lips parted on a trembling breath. "I'm afraid.''

"No reason," he said gently. His mouth brushed over her cheek, her ear. "I'm older. It's hard for me to lose control now. I won't do anything you don't want me to do." He smiled against her cool cheek. "No sex, honey. Just some very light love-making."

She lifted her eyes to his. "I want to," she said, letting him see the mingled hunger and apprehension.

"Remember who I am," he breathed, touching her hair. "I'm Gabriel. I'll never hurt you. Never."

She reached up and he bent to lift her, but he grimaced and had to set her down.

"Damn," he groaned, rubbing his arm and laughing through the pain. "Damned snake! It's still sore."

"Your poor arm," she said softly, touching it lightly. "I'm sorry."

"So am I," he sighed. "It's slowed me down a little."

She smiled. "I think I like that. For now, at least."

He glared at her, moving into the big armchair with slow ease. "Come here, then," he said, holding out his hand. "But watch where you touch."

"Prude," she accused, and actually laughed. It

was the first time she'd been able to joke in so long.

He drew her onto his hard thighs and shifted her so that her head lay against his shoulder. But instead of kissing her, he just sat, holding her. Outside, rain was beginning to come down. The room was dimly lit and cozy. Her eyes wandered around to the heavy oak desk, the large burgundy leather sofa, the long, wide matching divan, the huge bookcases against one wall and the wildlife paintings covering the other. It was a man's room. Gabe's room.

Closer, she heard his heartbeat, slow and heavy and regular at her ear, felt the sigh of his breath on her forehead. He smoothed her arm gently and his warm fingers felt good.

"It feels good, holding you," he said after a minute. He crossed one leg over the other, shifting her closer. "Comfortable?"

"Yes," she murmured drowsily, closing her eyes. She moved her hand experimentally on his broad chest and arm, feeling the bandage through the thin fabric of his shirt. "How long will it take to heal?" she asked.

"Not much longer, I hope," he muttered. "Damned fool, I should have looked where I was reaching. I dropped my rope behind the chute where we were working the small herd, and didn't look when I leaned over. The rattler got me right on the arm.''

She studied his face curiously. "I never heard what happened to the snake. Blood poisoning…?''

He glowered at her. "The snake went the way of most snakes that come too close to me. I took my rifle and shot him.''

"With snakebite?'' she gasped.

"I had the rifle right next to me,'' he admitted. "And just enough bad temper to do it before the poison started working. The boys got me to the emergency room, snake's head and all, and they gave me the antivenin. I was sicker than I want to remember for a couple of days. I'd just gotten back on my feet when you showed up with Mother.''

"And spoiled your recovery,'' she recalled, smiling.

"I wouldn't say that.'' He nuzzled his cheek over her hair. "I have to admit that you've brightened up the place. Nothing like having a woman around to get a man well.''

"You should have married,'' she murmured.

He lifted her left hand, noting the absence of a ring. "Becky's the one who's going to get hurt by the court suit, you know,'' he said unexpectedly, caressing her fingers gently with his. "From what

I saw today, her father won't care who he destroys to get that money.''

"Money always meant everything to him," she said. "He grew up poor. Really dirt-poor. But it warped him. He doesn't really care about anyone except himself."

"Stop feeling sorry for him," he chided. "People make their own hells, haven't you noticed? It isn't life that does the damage, Maggie; it's the way people react to it. Attitude is everything in this world."

"This, from a man whose attitude is to flatten anything that gets in his way?" she asked, eyebrows arching.

"It makes things simpler," he said, grinning.

She shook her head. "You always were too much man for any ordinary woman. I never thought you'd find a woman brave enough to take you on."

He stared at her for a long moment, his eyes thoughtful, curious. "Plenty have tried, as you might have gathered. Mother's done her best to supply me with a wife."

"She only wants happiness for you," Maggie said gently. "She doesn't like seeing you grow old all alone."

"Neither do I, sometimes." He brushed his

thumb over the palm of the hand he was holding, feeling its softness. "I want a son," he added, looking straight into her eyes.

She felt the wildest kind of excitement. He was only making a statement, she told herself, only expressing a buried desire. But the way he said it, and the way he looked at her, made her body burn to give him that child. She felt herself trembling and knew he could feel it, too.

"I wanted to talk to your attorneys while we were in the city," he said after a minute. "But I thought it was more important to get Becky out of that lunatic's reach. I'll fly back down on Monday and meet with them."

"But—"

"It doesn't do any good to argue with me," he said reasonably. "Haven't you discovered that by now?"

"I don't want to be taken over," she began.

"Sure you do, honey," he murmured, smiling gently as he folded her against his good side and eased her down in the big chair. "And this is as good a time as any to show you that you do."

"Gabri—"

The rest of his name was buried under his warm, ardent mouth. She sighed gently and closed her eyes, drinking in his strength and warmth and masculinity. He made her feel so small and vulnerable, so protected. Nothing would ever happen to her when Gabe was around.

His lean fingers trailed down her arm and suddenly, shockingly, onto her blouse.

"Don't," she whispered, catching his wrist.

"You let me do it before," he whispered back, brushing his hard mouth over hers. "You aren't going to tell me you don't enjoy it, are you?"

"It's...it isn't...right," she faltered, searching for the words that would express what she felt.

He lifted his head and looked into her eyes. "Because I'll think you're easy?" he asked matter-of-factly. "Now that's a hell of a misconception. I know plenty about you, Maggie Turner. What I know best is that you've had a rough time with men and that you're about as clued up as a pretty kid at a carnival. Do you think I'm callous enough to play around with you under those circumstances?"

The question floored her. She hadn't expected such a blunt explanation.

"No," she had to answer him honestly. "No, I don't think you're callous."

"Then let go of my wrist, sweet, and let me show you how good it feels to have my hand on your warm skin,'' he breathed, smiling as he bent again to her mouth.

He was a bulldozer, she thought dimly. A human, blue-eyed bulldozer with a mouth as sweet as mountain honey. He opened her lips with his and pushed his tongue gently into her mouth, feeling her stiffen at the new intimacy.

''Give it a chance,'' he whispered. ''Deep kisses are an acquired taste. Let me.''

She hesitated for an instant but then she gave in, letting his tongue invade her mouth. It was frightening, the sudden explosion of feeling that the searching motion caused in her body. She stiffened again, but not in rejection; she moaned, gripping his hard arms.

Meanwhile, one lean hand had moved the fabric of her blouse aside and was sliding warmly under it and around her. She felt the clasp of her bra give suddenly and the cool breeze of the room on her bare flesh. Her nipple hardened even as his fingers began to search teasingly at the edge of her breast, lightly exploring.

Her breath sounded odd. It caught in her throat and sighed out in little gasps. He heard it and smiled even through his own wild excitement.

''God, you set me on fire,'' he murmured, lifting his head as his hands slid around her and under her breasts, holding their warm, soft weight as he stared directly into her shocked eyes. His thumbs edged up, and she shuddered as they found and tested the tiny peaks of her breasts. "I'm not hurting you, am I?" he asked softly. "I haven't touched a woman like this for a long time."

"It doesn't hurt," she said, her voice husky.

He looked down and expertly lifted the bra away so that her breasts were revealed, small and high and very firm. "Yes," he said with a kind of reverence. "Yes, this is how I pictured you, all the long years in between: sweet, pretty little breasts so soft and warm in my hands—"

"Gabriel!" she burst out, shocked by his intimate description of her.

"Don't cover them," he whispered, bending to her parted lips. "Let me look at you. Let me touch you. We're both adults, Maggie. We're hurting no one."

He had such a silky, deep voice. It hypnotized her. She stayed very still, trembling softly as he caressed her mouth with his lips. His hands cupped her, testing her softness, adoring her womanliness.

She felt her body stretching, arching upward to savor what he was doing to it. Her head fell back, her eyes half-closed. She was sixteen again, burning for him, aching for his body. Dennis and all unpleasantness was pushed to the back of her mind, while Gabe held her body in ardent bondage.

He lifted his lips from hers and looked down, watching her body plead. "Yes," he whispered. "I want that, too, Maggie."

He bent, lifting her against his arm, and softly brushed his mouth over the very tip of her breast. She whimpered. Her fingers caught in his hair, tugging gently.

"You're trembling all over," he breathed. "I've never in my life felt so hungry for a woman."

As he spoke, he opened his mouth and put it completely over one soft, pretty breast. She felt the warm, moist darkness envelop her, and she arched even further to give him total access to her, trembling as his mouth fed on her softness, bit at her, tasted her. Her mind hardly worked at all, drowning in sensation.

His hand slid down her back to her hips and drew them suddenly under his, then he turned her in the big chair so she could feel the pressure of his arousal.

Her eyes opened to look up into his. She shuddered, but she didn't try to move away. "I hated it…when that happened to Dennis. Why is it…so beautiful with you?" she whispered tearfully.

He couldn't answer her. His mind was in turmoil, his body in anguish. He bent again to her sweet mouth and kissed it as if he'd die trying to get enough. Despite the sore arm, he lifted her close, fighting his shirt out of the way so he could feel her soft breasts against his chest.

She cried out, shocked at the sensations she felt. Never with Dennis, never like this. She wanted him. She wanted to lie down and feel his weight on her body; she wanted total union with him.

Time seemed to slow, to stand still. She was crying, and when the world came into focus again, he was comforting her with the most exquisite kind of tenderness.

"Shh," he breathed into her mouth. "Shh, calm down now. It's all right, calm down." He pressed her hot cheek against his chest and rocked her, gently smoothed his hands along her back, easing away the passion between them. "That's my girl," he whispered. "Just be still."

"I feel so strange," she whispered unsteadily.

"So do I." He laughed gently. "Would you like to know where?"

"Hush," she mumbled, hiding her hot face.

He ran his fingers through her thick short hair, testing its silkiness. "Were you frightened of what was happening?" he asked softly.

"A little," she told him.

His fingers touched her ear, sending delicious thrills through her sensitized nerves. "Eventually, I'll have to know."

"Know…what?" she hesitated.

"Whether or not you're capable of giving in to me completely," he replied. His chest, beneath her bare breasts, rose and fell heavily. "This kind of thing gets unmanageable pretty quickly, Maggie. For Becky's sake, we can't have an illicit relationship. You see that, I hope."

Things were going too fast. She stood up, tugging her blouse together, and stared down at him. "It's too soon," she said, wary.

"No, I don't think it is." He watched her fumble with buttons. He didn't bother with his own, merely sprawled back in the chair, his broad, hair-covered chest bare and welcoming, his mouth swollen and sensuous and smiling with pure male appreciation of her. "You'd better start seeing it that way, too, honey. You're going to need some help when you get into court. Especially now, with your ex-husband's scandalous opinion of our relationship."

"I'll deny it."

He lifted an eyebrow. "By all means," he suggested, and picked up his brandy snifter. "His attorney will get you on the stand and ask if you and

I have ever been intimate, you'll blush like somebody's embarrassed child, and he'll have Becky.''

That was true, but it didn't help her pride. She finished fastening her blouse and glared at him. "What do you propose to do about it—marry me?" she asked with faint sarcasm.

"Why not?" he replied casually, and took a sip of brandy. "You're pretty and honest, you've got a lovely little girl, and I'm a lonely man. You need money, I've got it. We're a match made in heaven.''

"Those aren't good reasons to get married," she returned, but she felt as if the ground had been cut from under her. She wanted him. Physically, at least. He attracted her, and perhaps she wouldn't freeze in his arms. He was strong and powerful and rich. He'd take care of them both, of Becky and herself. And in bed, he'd give her what she'd never had with a man. But why was he offering? He wasn't a marrying man, he'd said it before. What did he expect to get out of it? Or did he just want Maggie so much that he was willing to give up his freedom to have her? That didn't make a lot of sense, either. It would be a risk, marrying him. What if it didn't work out?

The turbulence of her thoughts showed in her face as she looked at him.

"Go ahead," he said, "torment yourself with what-ifs." He finished the brandy. "You've got a little longer to play on the line before I start reeling you in." He got to his feet and towered over her. "Just remember, honey, I make a hell of an adversary. I won't give up or give in. If I want you, I'll have you."

"By force?" she demanded with a bit of her old spirit.

"Never by force, pretty girl," he replied. He bent and brushed his mouth over hers. "I want to ravish your senses, not take something you don't want to give me. Physical pleasure has to be shared, or it's selfish. You've had enough of that already."

She searched his eyes, afraid of him, hungry for him. "Can it be shared, Gabriel?" she asked in a whisper, her eyes wide and curious.

"If both partners are intent on giving more than they expect to get," he said enigmatically.

"And it...isn't supposed to hurt?"

His eyes burned down into hers. "No," he bit off. "It isn't supposed to hurt. Ever."

She dropped her gaze to his bare chest. "I didn't know. There was no one I could ask, you see. Even my best friend, Trudie. I can't talk about things like that."

"Except with me, apparently," he mused, his eyes gently indulgent. He caught her hand in his. "Sit down."

He dropped down onto the big sofa and let her curl up next to him again as he lit a cigarette. "I hope you're not sleepy. This may take a while. Don't look at me, if it helps. I'm going to tell you all about sex, Miss Turner. I think it's time, don't you?"

She looked up at him, feeling her face color. "I know…"

"Nothing," he said for her, grinning. "But you will when I'm through. Now be quiet and listen."

It was fascinating. He might have been a university lecturer giving a cram course in sex education. He did it without vulgarity, in a matter-of-fact way that didn't embarrass or shock her. And when he was through, she knew more than marriage and having a child had taught her.

She caught her breath. "I never realized it was so complicated," she told him.

"It's a miracle," he replied. "In every respect. And miracles shouldn't be twisted into minor amusements. The only times I ever had sex with women, I was involved emotionally. I couldn't lower my pride enough to buy it."

And men were supposed to be indifferent about

feelings? She stared up at him, fascinated. "Did you learn...all that...with women?"

The corners of his firm mouth curved up. "Not all of it, no. I wanted to be a doctor when I graduated from high school. I took two years of premed before I switched to veterinary science. I learned all sorts of interesting things about bodies and how they work."

"So I've noticed," she murmured.

He touched her chin, tilting it. "Sex is beautiful," he said softly. "In the proper circumstances, it's an exquisite expression of love and commitment. God must have thought so, because He allowed children to come of it."

She searched his pale eyes, smiling. He was an enigma. Such a hard, unbending man to be so sensitive. "Thank you for the lesson," she said.

"My pleasure. Hearing it might not remove those scars, but it could put what you've experienced into perspective. You aren't frigid; you're just untaught."

"I could never talk to Dennis about sex," she recalled quietly. "He said it was my fault that it was never good."

"I'm afraid he had it backward," he replied. "A considerate lover can make it good."

Her eyes lifted. Her lips parted to ask the question, but at the last second she got cold feet and averted her eyes.

He leaned close to her ear. "What do you want to know, big eyes? How I am in bed?"

"Of course not!" she blurted.

He took her earlobe gently between his teeth and teased it, and she felt the sensations all the way to her toes. "I'm slow, and thorough, and I know where all the nerves are," he whispered.

She made a wild little sound and darted away from him, her eyes like saucers in a face burning with embarrassment.

He laughed, leaning back against the sofa to study her frenzied confusion. "Running away so soon?" he murmured. "You wanted to know. I told you."

"You were being kind, for once," she grumbled. "Now you're back to your old cutting self."

"I'm frustrated," he replied. "I should have explained frustration to you. It makes bears out of nice men."

"You never were a nice man," she told him, brushing back her hair.

"That's true," he agreed pleasantly. He winked at her. "But I'm sexy."

She smiled. "I guess you are," she agreed unexpectedly.

He lifted an eyebrow. "I'm delighted that you agree. At some future date, would you like me to prove it to you?"

"Well..."

"Chicken," he chided. "Go to bed. Tomorrow, I'm taking Becky for her first ride. You can come, if you like."

"Gabe, she's so small," she protested.

"And I'm big," he replied. "And I'll take good care of her. And her mother."

"I can't help being overprotective," she said defensively.

"It's just a stage you're going through," he told her. "You'll outgrow it. I'll help. Now, scoot. Let me drink myself to sleep, so that I can forget this swollen arm you damn near burst."

"I damn near burst?" she echoed blankly.

"Trying to rape me," he replied with virtuous indignation. "Look at me, for God's sake! Shirt half off, fingerprints all over my chest, I smell of whatever kind of perfume you've bathed in..."

Her eyes widened. He was flirting with her. She'd had so little experience with flirting. But it seemed like fun.

"You took my blouse off," she countered. "Women have equal rights."

"I took more than your blouse off, actually,"

he mused, staring at her breasts. "The ancient Greek women used to go bare-breasted, did you know? You'd have knocked the competition dead."

And she'd always thought of herself as too small to appeal to a man. Her fascinated gaze held his. "Do you really think so?"

He laughed softly. "Yes, I really think so. Go to bed, damn it. How long do you think I can sit here calmly talking about your breasts without stripping you and throwing you down on the carpet?"

"How uncivilized," she commented haughtily.

"Exciting." His eyes glittered wickedly. "Your bare back on that rug, and my body grinding you down into it with the door unlocked...."

She turned, catching her breath. "I'm going to bed."

"I wish I was going with you," he sighed, reaching for his brandy snifter. "Maggie..."

She paused, her hand on the doorknob. "Yes?"

"I want a few days to see how Becky adjusts. Then, if she likes it, you and I will talk and come to a decision about what needs doing."

She stared into his narrowed, quiet eyes. "I don't understand."

"Oh, I think you do," he said, and held her gaze

until her heartbeat shook her. "I think you know exactly what I mean, after tonight."

She held on to her nerves with shaky control. "I may not be able to give you what you want," she said. "Dennis…changed me. What we've done is sweet, and I like it. But…"

"But you aren't certain you can give yourself to me, is that it?" he asked with quiet perception.

"That's it exactly," she said miserably.

He pursed his lips to search her eyes. "Maggie, if it helps, I'm not insensitive to what you must feel about intimacy. But I think you're overlooking one important factor."

"What?"

"I'm not your ex-husband," he said. "I've never hurt a woman deliberately. I'm not a sadistic man."

"Oh, I know that," she told him. "I've always known that."

"Then give me credit for a little sensitivity," he replied. "Trust me."

"Trust is hard."

"Tell me about it." He chuckled darkly. "Or have you forgotten that I've had some hard knocks of my own in that department? Mother told you that I got hurt, but I'm the only one who knows how badly. I loved her. Or thought I did," he added, and for the first time he wasn't really sure. It all seemed very far away now, with Maggie here, lovely and tempting.

"I'm sorry about that."

"I'm sorry about your rough time, too, honey," he said softly. "But that's in the past. You and I have Becky to think about. If we don't do something, you may lose her."

"I know," she murmured.

"Don't worry," he said. "He'll have to go through me to get her, court or no court. But maybe there's an easier way. I've got an idea. I'll tell you if it pans out. Good night."

"I haven't even thanked you," she said suddenly, "for all you've done."

His eyes traveled slowly to her mouth. "Haven't you?" He raised the snifter, smiling as she turned, flustered, and left him there.

Chapter Six

Becky seemed like a different child on the big ranch. Despite the demands of his position, and his sore arm, Gabe found time to help her get used to her new environment.

He put her on a horse the day after she arrived, while Maggie stood with her hands clenched, murmuring soft prayers.

"It's all right, honey," Gabe told the nervous little girl as he helped her onto a small mare, grimacing as he forced his arm to perform the minor task. Becky was light, but any pressure still caused him some problems. "She's old and gentle. Your mother used to ride her, in fact," he added, glancing toward Maggie with a grin. "Remember Butterball?"

"That isn't Butterball!" Maggie exclaimed. "But Gabe, she'd have to be twenty-five years old."

"She's twenty-six," he said. He checked the cinch and put the reins in Becky's hands, teaching her how to sit the horse, how to hold it in check, how to keep her knees and elbows in and guide the horse with the faintest pressure of her legs.

"You sure know a lot about horses," Becky said with shy admiration, her soft green eyes glancing off his.

"I've worked around them all my life," he replied. "I love animals. I took courses in veterinary science in college and almost had a degree in it."

"I like animals, too," Becky said enthusiastically. "But we never got to have any," she added, looking away sadly. "Daddy was allergic. And when we came away, Mama had to work and I had to go away to school. They don't let you have dogs at school."

"Do you want a dog?" Gabe asked her, ignoring Maggie's frantic signals and head shaking. "Because Bill Dane down the road has a litter of registered collies. If you want one, I'll get it for you."

Becky's face was fascinating—a study in admiration, excitement, surprise and pure delight. "You would?" she whispered.

Maggie shut up. She'd let the dog sleep in the parlor. She'd buy it a house. Whatever she had to do, it would be worth it to see that young face so happy. She hadn't even known Becky wanted a pet.

"I would," Gabe said, and grinned. "If your mother doesn't mind," he added belatedly, cocking an eyebrow at Maggie.

"Of course her mother doesn't mind," Maggie murmured, and made a face at him.

He laughed. "I thought you wouldn't. Closing the gate after the bull gets out, don't they say," he added.

"I like dogs," she said.

"Me too!" Becky burst out, her ponytail bobbing as she stared down at Gabe. She started to reach out but abruptly brought her hand back to her reins, and her small face closed up all over again.

Maggie felt tears sting her eyes. She'd have to tell him, later, how great a step that was for Becky, who avoided any physical contact with people she didn't know—especially men. Just the inclination to reach out was a milestone in the child's life.

But he seemed to know, because when he

looked toward Maggie he wasn't laughing. And the eyes that met hers were dark with a kind of pain.

"Can we go now? Right now?" Becky asked excitedly. "Can we get a puppy today?"

"First we go riding," Gabe said. "Then we'll see."

"All right," Becky sighed.

"Becky," Maggie chided. "Where are your manners?"

"In my back pocket." Becky grinned. "Want to see?"

It was a sharp and delightful change to see her shy little daughter so vividly happy and outgoing. Maggie smiled up at Gabe, the sunlight turning her eyes as green as grass.

He winked at her before he turned to give her the reins of her own mount. "Can you get up all by yourself?" he asked in a gently mocking tone of voice.

She glared at him. "I know how to ride," she replied indignantly—and then ruined everything by missing the stirrup.

He caught her arm with his good hand and kept her upright. "Pilgrim," he accused. He steadied her while she got her booted foot into the stirrup and threw the other leg over gracefully. The steely hand on her arm wasn't doing a lot for her nerves, but she didn't refuse the offer of assistance.

He gathered the reins of his own horse and stepped easily into the saddle, looking so much at home up there that Maggie just stared at him.

"Stay right with me, honey," Gabe told Becky, moving into step with her horse. "There's nothing to worry about. I'll take care of you."

"All right," Becky said. Her small hands gripped the reins just as Gabe had taught her to. She glanced at him to make sure she was doing it right, and he nodded.

Maggie trailed along beside Gabe on the wide farm road, drinking in the beauty of vast horizons and grazing cattle and the feel of the warm spring breeze in her hair. There had been other times like this, long ago, when she and his sisters had gone riding. Sometimes they'd meet him unexpectedly on the trail, and her heart would run wild. It might have been only a schoolgirl crush, but it had hurt when she hadn't seen him again. Her eyes adored him unconsciously, admiring the powerful length of his body, the straightness of his carriage, the lean hands so deft and strong on the reins. He was exceptional. He always had been. And she might marry him....

The thought disturbed her. She'd been wrong

about Dennis. What if she was wrong about Gabe? It was different, living with someone. You never knew people until you lived with them.

He turned his head, studying her in a somber silence. "You're too quiet," he said. "Say something."

"She's always quiet," Becky told him. "She doesn't talk much."

"She used to," Gabe returned with a grin. "She never shut up, in fact."

"I only blabbered because you made me nervous," she shot back, and then cleared her throat when she realized what she'd confessed.

"Your mama had a crush on me," Gabe said arrogantly, lifting his chin at a cocky angle as he studied Maggie with knowing eyes. "She thought I was the best thing since buttered bread."

Becky giggled, and Becky's mama ground her teeth together. "Why didn't you marry my mama, Uncle Gabe?" Becky asked suddenly.

Maggie wanted to get under the horse. She bit her lower lip while Gabe stared at her under the wide brim of his hat and pursed his lips thoughtfully.

"I was afraid she wouldn't be happy with what I had to offer her, back then," he said matter-of-factly and without embarrassment. "We weren't always well-to-do, young lady,'' he added with a gentle smile. "We had some hard times here for a while. It was during those hard times that I lost track of your mother.''

Maggie stared at him, fascinated. Was it just for Becky's benefit—a little white lie—or was he telling the truth?

He caught her intent scrutiny and grinned, his pale eyes making a joke of it. She smiled back, but something inside her closed up like a flower in the darkness: she'd wanted it to be true.

"Down this way," Gabe said suddenly, turning Becky's mare. "I've got something to show you.''

There was a little path down to the creek, and near it were several cows with calves.

"Baby cows!" Becky burst out. "Could I pet one?''

"Oh, Gabe, no, those are longhorn cows!'' protested Maggie, who'd once been chased by a mad mama longhorn.

"These are old pets," Gabe replied easily, dismounting. "They won't hurt her. Come on, baby.''

He reached up his arms. Becky hesitated, but in the end she let him swing her to the ground. And this time he made sure she didn't see him grimace.

"These are just a few weeks old," he told her, keeping between the young girl and the old cows.

"Go easy, now. You can win over most any crea-
ture if you're just slow and careful and talk soft.
Ask your mama."

Maggie blushed furiously as he glanced over his
shoulder with a mischievous grin.

Mercifully, Becky didn't understand what he
was saying. Her wide eyes were on the calves. She
moved close to a young one and touched it between the eyes, where it was silky. It tried to nibble
on her hand, and she jerked back with a delighted
laugh.

"Oh, isn't she pretty?" Becky cooed, doing it
again.

"He," Gabe corrected. "That youngster is going to grow up to be a good young bull."

"Not a steer?" Maggie asked.

"Not this one. See the conformation?" he
asked, gesturing toward the smooth lines of the
young animal. "He's already breaking weight-gain
ratio records. I want to breed this one."

"How do you keep up with so many cattle?"
Becky asked unexpectedly.

"I have a big computer in my office," he told
her. "I have every cow and calf I own in it. Ranching is moving into the twentieth century, honey.
We don't use tally books too much anymore."

"What's a tally book?"

He explained it to her, about the old-time method of counting cattle, about the days when every ranch owner would send a rep to roundup to make sure none of his cattle were being appropriated.

"That's still done in these parts, too," he added, leaning against a tree to smoke a cigarette while Becky stroked the calf. "We have quite a crowd here when we start branding and moving cattle, and at the end of it I throw a big barbecue for the neighbors. We help each other out, even on a ranch this size."

"Do you really use those airplanes to round up cattle?" Maggie asked.

"Sure. The helicopter, too. It's a great time-saver when you're moving thousands of head." His pale eyes moved slowly down Maggie's body, over the white knit short-sleeved sweater and the neat jeans that hugged her rounded hips and long, elegant legs.

"It's hard work, too," she said, burning under his frank appraisal.

"Very hard." He lifted the cigarette to his mouth, glancing at Becky, who was talking softly to the calf while its mother watched with indulgent interest. "I get ill-tempered this time of year."

"I did notice," Maggie began.

He turned, crushing out the cigarette as he started toward her. "Did you?"

She backed up. Surely he wouldn't...not with Becky watching!

He intimidated her back against a large oak tree and kept her there with just his presence. "What was that," he asked politely, "about noticing I was ill-tempered?"

"You would have sent me packing, but for your mother," she reminded him.

"Not really." He smiled at her gently. "You started getting under my skin all over again, that first day. I might have let you get as far as packing, but I'd have found an excuse to keep you here."

Her heart began to run wild. Becky wasn't even watching.

Gabe moved a little closer, leaning one arm, the uninjured one, beside her head against the tree. The action brought him so close that she could smell the tobacco on his breath, feel the muscles cording in his powerful legs and chest.

His eyes dropped to her mouth. "I can almost taste the coffee on your breath," he whispered. "And if Becky was a few yards down the creek, I'd ease my body down on yours and let you feel the effect you have on me in those tight little jeans."

Her breath caught. "Gabriel!"

"Don't try to pretend you don't know it, either," he continued. His eyes dropped. "That sweater doesn't hide what you're feeling."

Maggie frowned slightly. Her eyes followed his, and she could see the tautness in her nipples even through the flimsy bra and knit top.

"You know, don't you, that your body reflects desire that way?" he whispered, searching her wide eyes. "Why do you think men get so stirred by a woman who isn't wearing a bra?"

"I...I am wearing one," she began.

"It doesn't cover much, does it?" He frowned. "Don't go around the men that way," he added suddenly. "I can't afford to fire anybody this week."

Her eyebrows arched. "But—"

"You have pretty breasts," he whispered softly, holding her eyes.

She tingled from head to toe. Her breath wouldn't let out. Gabe's eyes were drowning her, she couldn't get to the surface. The whole world was pale blue, and her body was trembling slightly, burning up inside. Her lips parted, and she made a soft, barely perceptible movement toward him.

"You shouldn't talk that way to me," she breathed.

"You shouldn't let me," he whispered back. "If you keep encouraging me, I'll make love to you."

"You can't."

"Sure I can." He nuzzled her nose with his. "So can you. I don't mind if you sleep with me."

"There's Becky."

He smiled. "Becky is quite a girl. She'll make a rancher before she quits."

"That isn't what I meant," Maggie replied. She touched his chest, liking the feel of hard muscle under the warm shirt. "You're very hairy there," she said absently, and caught her breath when she remembered how his chest felt against her bare skin.

"You always seemed to like that," he murmured, watching her. "At least you sure stared when I stripped off my shirt while I was working."

She swallowed. "You...you're very nicely built."

He smiled. "So are you."

Maggie smiled back. She felt shy and giddy, all at once.

They stared at each other for a long moment, eyes meeting eyes, curious and then quiet and probing and intense. She felt her breath quicken, saw his chest rise and fall heavily.

"I'm on fire," he whispered huskily. "I want your hands on my bare skin."

She trembled because she wanted it, too. "We…aren't alone."

"How fortunate for you," he replied curtly. "Because if we were, I'd lay you down, so help me."

Her body reacted to his threat in a wildly responsive way. She tried to get a deep breath and couldn't.

"No comment?" he asked. "No urge to cut and run? Or doesn't the thought of having sex with me frighten you anymore?"

"It would be…more…than that," she whispered. "Wouldn't it?"

"More than you can imagine, honey," he replied evenly, searching her soft eyes. "You and I would go up in flames if we got in bed together."

Her mind was seeing that. Seeing his long, nude body stretching against hers on cool, striped sheets, feeling his muscles ripple as her hands smoothed over them and savored their warm, rough strength.

"My God, don't look at me like that," he cried harshly, and actually shuddered. "I can read your mind!"

Her lips parted on a trembling breath. "So beautiful," she murmured. "That…with you."

Gabe caught her arm with his hand, holding it with such fierce ardor that she welcomed the discomfort. Her head tilted back, her mouth invited his.

"I can't kiss you like that with Becky here," he said in a hoarse undertone. "God, I couldn't even stop once I started! I'd devour you."

"I'd let you," she whispered softly. "I'd let you do anything...."

He turned away with a hard groan, letting go of her arm. "Becky, want to see the wildflowers?" he called. His voice didn't seem quite normal but Becky didn't notice. She was still petting the calf with fascination.

"Sure!" she called back, laughing.

Maggie eased away from the tree on shaky legs. She wasn't at all sure how to handle these new, explosive emotions. Gabe was wearing her down without even trying. And now she wanted him, as she hadn't even in her youth. She couldn't think what was best anymore. She wasn't at all sure that she could leave him.

"Come on, slowpoke," Gabe called to her, smiling, although his eyes were blazing as they met hers. "Let's get going."

She waited for him to boost her into the saddle after he'd helped Becky up. But he was towering over her, so close that she could feel the warmth of his body.

"I've got to," he whispered sharply as Becky turned her horse away from them. "Just for a second!"

His mouth crushed down on hers, hungrily, roughly. She opened her lips, but he drew back immediately with a visible shudder.

"Oh..." she whispered on a sob.

"I'll be on my knees by tonight," he ground out, helping her into the saddle. "My God, I'm already shaking like a boy."

"So am I," she told him with an unsteady smile.

"Pretty soon we're going to have to settle this thing, honey," he said, his eyes steady and intent. "I can't handle what I feel."

Her face colored. "I can't be sure—"

"I won't rush you," he interrupted as Becky came back toward them. "Good girl," he called, striding toward his horse. "You're beginning to look like a cowgirl!"

"Am I really?" Becky asked enthusiastically.

"You really are," he assured her. "I'm going to show you a sea of wildflowers. Texas meadows look like fairyland in spring."

He led them back toward the farm road, then turned to the south. They were facing a field that looked as if it had been paint-splattered. It was alive with color.

"The blue is bluebonnets, our state flower," he announced, sweeping his hand toward the distant horizon, where dust clouds told them men were massing cattle. "The orange and red is Mexican hat and Indian paintbrush, and there are daisies and some blooming thornbushes mixed in with it. All this used to be prairie," he added with a wistful look. "Black with buffalo herds, unspoiled. It's a pity what we have to trade for progress."

"Will the buffalo come back?" Becky asked.

Gabe leaned his forearms over the pommel and shook his head. The leather creaked with the smooth motion of his body. "Afraid not, honey. They're gone, like the pioneers and the Indians. Gone in a rage of passion called westward expansion."

"Reactionary," Maggie accused gently. "You'd like to tear up the cities and start over."

He turned toward her. "Sure I would." He grinned. "I'm a cattleman. I like plenty of space and no fences."

"You were born a hundred years too late."

"Amen to that," he agreed. He sighed, glancing toward the dust. "Well, I hate to do it, but I'll have to get you two home so that I can go back to work.

Becky, we'll go over to Dane's late this afternoon and see about that pup. What do you say?''

The child grinned. "I think you're terrific, Uncle Gabe."

"Do you like it here, honey?" he asked, suddenly serious.

"Oh, yes," Becky sighed, her face radiant as she stared around. "I wish I could live here always."

He looked over her head at Maggie, whose own eyes dropped. She didn't know if she could give him what he'd demand if she married him. Marriage terrified her, he had to know that. Please, she thought, please don't back me into a corner.

He seemed to understand what she was feeling, because he didn't say another word about it. Instead, he began talking about puppies again, and on this happy topic Becky kept up an enthusiastic monologue all the way home.

The days went quickly after that. Gabe always found time to spend with Becky and her mother. He bought the collie puppy for Becky and convinced her that they had to wait until it was weaned to bring it home. It was only for a few days, and he kept the little girl busy with all sorts of adventures.

He found a bird's nest for her to explore one

day. The next, he drove her and Maggie in the truck to a small creek that ran right across a dirt road, where Becky could wade and chase butterflies that lifted in swirls of color from the damp sand. He always had a surprise for Becky. And like any child, she responded to his attention with slow but genuine affection. As time passed, she relaxed and actually seemed to trust him. Maggie, whose own feelings for Gabe had fluctuated wildly from anger to affection, was having trouble adjusting to his sudden switch in attitude toward her. Becky was getting all the attention now. Gabe hadn't made a move toward her physically since the day they'd gone riding. He seemed to be deliberately letting things cool off between them. He was gentle with her, and he teased her and picked at her in a roughly affectionate way. But he hadn't made another pass at her, and although it was a kind of relief in one way, it was a bitter disappointment in another. Maggie couldn't begin to understand herself these days.

Things were going along fine when a phone call came for her one day while Janet and Gabe were out. It was from her attorney in San Antonio, telling her that Dennis had initiated the custody suit. And as she'd dreaded, he'd named Gabe as her lover, claiming that she was unfit to raise a child when she was openly living with a man in an illicit fashion.

Maggie was devastated. She didn't mention it to the family, but Gabe seemed to sense something was wrong. He watched her as they went to get Becky's pup, his eyes narrowed and thoughtful.

"He's filed, hasn't he?" he asked under his breath when Becky cuddled the pup on the way back home.

"Yes," she said miserably, glancing over the seat of his Lincoln to the happy little girl in the back seat. "I don't know how to tell her."

"Leave that to me," he said gently. "I'll handle it. Just relax, Miss Butterball. You're going to be fine. So is Becky." And he began to whistle as if he hadn't a care in the world. But Maggie was beginning to understand him now. And she knew he had something up his sleeve.

Becky carried her collie into the house with almost comical care, cuddling it and telling it not to be afraid. It was a sable-and-white female, and Becky was on top of the world. She showed the tiny animal to the whole household, delighted when Janet asked to hold it and cuddled it warmly. She could hardly bear to put it down long enough to have supper. It was fascinating, the change that small animal was making in the shy, withdrawn child. In fact, Maggie mused, watching her, the change Becky and Gabe had made in each other was amazing. The cold, taciturn man and the shy child had lit candles each for the other. They were both changing, day by day; opening up, warming. Janet had mentioned it to Maggie, who was seeing it at even closer range.

Becky walked up to Gabe when it was time for her to go to bed and looked at him with worshiping eyes.

"I wish you were my father," she said with such wistfulness in her voice that Gabe's face actually softened.

He hesitated for a minute, studying the delicate little face with a curious, searching expression. He glanced at Maggie and seemed to come to a decision about something.

He went down on one knee, so that he could see Becky's eyes. "I'm not always going to be pleasant," he said matter-of-factly, talking to her as if she were an adult. "I have a temper. I lose it. Sometimes I get impatient with people, and there are times when I want to be alone. I may hurt your feelings sometimes without realizing it. You might wish you'd never come here."

Becky nodded, clutching the puppy to her chest.

"I have bad days, too," she said very somberly. "But I like you even when you're mad."

He laughed softly. "I like you, too. So how do you feel about staying here?"

"You mean, like a vacation?"

He shook his head. "I mean permanently."

Becky stared at him while Maggie held her breath. "Would you be my daddy?" she asked softly.

Gabe's jaw tautened. "Yes."

Becky nibbled on her lower lip. There was a little fear left. But even as Maggie watched, it seemed to drain away. "My daddy was bad to me," she whispered. "He made me afraid. But I know you wouldn't ever hurt me."

"Oh, God," he breathed huskily, emotion in his voice, his whole look. "No, I'd never hurt you, precious."

Tears spilled over Becky's eyes. "Oh, Uncle Gabe, I love you!"

She threw her free arm around the big man's neck and nuzzled her little face against his. Gabe held her, but he didn't speak. Not for a long time.

"I'll take care of you, Becky," he said at last, his voice oddly taut. "You and your mama. Nobody will ever hurt you again."

Becky kissed his hard cheek. "I'll take care of

you, too,'' she promised, smiling. She drew back
and frowned. ''Uncle Gabe, your eyes are wet.''

''I guess they are,'' he said without embarrassment, and grinned. ''It isn't every day that a man
gets a new daughter.''

''Could I call you Father?'' she asked.

''Anytime at all.''

Becky glanced at her mother, whose eyes were
also a little wet. ''Can we stay with my new
daddy?'' she asked softly.

''Darling, of course we can,'' Maggie said with
feeling. She met Gabe's eyes. ''Of course we
can!''

He nodded, his eyes never leaving hers.
''Mother!'' he called.

Janet came out of the living room in a rush.
''What is it! Is something wrong? I was just watching a movie—''

''Maggie and I are getting married,'' he told her
without preamble. ''How about arranging everything?''

Janet looked as if she might faint. ''What?''

''We're getting married,'' Gabe said curtly.

''We really are,'' Maggie assured her, smiling.
She turned to Becky. ''Darling, go on up to bed,
and I'll be right there to tuck you in. Oh, the
dog…''

"It's all right," Janet said. "I had Jennie put a nice wooden box with a blanket by the bed." She smiled warmly. "Becky, I'm going to be your grannie!"

"I'll be so good," Becky promised, going close to her grandmother. "You'll be proud of me, I promise."

"I always was," Janet laughed. She stared from Maggie to Gabe, all smiles. "What a delightful surprise!"

"Surprise, my eye," Gabe said disgustedly, glaring at her. "But you got your own way. As usual." Janet's pleasure dissipated a little with that cutting remark. Gabe brushed by Maggie on his way back upstairs. "We'll talk later," he said. "Come on, Becky, I'll go up with you."

"Yes, sir," Becky said smartly, and ruined it all with a large, mischievous grin. She cuddled her puppy and giggled as it licked her cheek.

"Oh, Maggie, I'm delighted," Janet sighed, hugging her. "If you knew how your mother and I hoped for this one day."

"It isn't all what it seems," Maggie said gently. "It's mostly for Becky. Gabe says I wouldn't have a prayer in court as things stand. Dennis has remarried."

"I know. But it will work out for the best. Re-

ally it will. I only wish my son could forgive me
for the past," she added wistfully. "Maybe it will
happen someday."

"Of course it will," Maggie assured her. "Janet,
am I doing the right thing?" she added, glancing
worriedly up the stairs. "For Becky, of course it
is. But I...don't love Gabe. And he doesn't love
me."

"Love comes after marriage sometimes," Janet
said. "Give it time, darling. Just give it time."

Maggie nodded, but she was worried, and not
just about the distant future. Gabriel was going to
want a physical commitment from her. And despite
the desire she felt for him, she wasn't at all sure
she was going to be able to give in to him—marriage or no marriage.

She occupied her mind by taking a minute to
call Trudie in London, with Gabe's permission, to
tell her the news.

Her boss was delighted for her, even though she
hated losing her only employee. She made Maggie
promise to write her all about it, then launched into
delightful details of her European trip. She added
that it must be nice to marry a man who could
allow his intended transatlantic phone calls.

Maggie agreed that it was, but all the while she
was talking about how wonderful it would be for

Becky, she worried about what she was walking
into. Gabe had been so good to Becky, and to Maggie. He deserved more than gratitude. He deserved
a wife who could love him and take care of him
and be everything he needed in bed. Would she be
able to live up to all that, ever? Or would he regret
his impulsive decision to marry her?

Chapter Seven

Gabe had to go out with one of his men to see about a sick bull—a purebred one, apparently, from the worried look on his face—and he still wasn't back when Janet went up to bed, humming delightedly.

Maggie curled up on the sofa in the living room, tucking the full skirt of her candy-striped shirtwaist dress around her slender legs and bare feet. She was halfheartedly watching television when he returned, and her eyes were drawn immediately to the sight of him standing in the doorway.

He always looked different when he was in casual clothes. His denim jeans clung lovingly to the powerful muscles of his long legs. The chambray shirt outlined every hard contour of his chest and arms. The wide-brimmed hat he wore gave his face enticing shadows, and the boots made him even taller than he actually was. Maggie could never get enough of just looking at him. He was so virile, such a—a *man.*

"I hoped you'd still be up," he said, closing the door behind him. As an afterthought he locked it, then, with a wicked smile, stood watching Maggie's disturbed expression as he shucked off the thick leather gloves he was wearing and tossed them aside, along with his hat. "Nervous of me, Margaret?" he taunted gently.

She felt her breath lodge in her throat as he came closer. "A little," she said. Why try to deny it? Those pale, narrowed eyes saw altogether too much.

"Why? Because I locked the door?"

"Everyone's gone upstairs...to bed," she faltered.

He stopped just in front of her and searched her green eyes quietly. "I don't want to be interrupted while we're talking."

"What are we going to talk about?" she asked hesitantly.

He pursed his lips and reached for a cigarette. "Why you're afraid of me, for one thing."

"I'm just nervous," she corrected. "Not afraid."

"They're usually one and the same." He went to the television and switched it off, then came back and dropped down beside her, pulling an ashtray forward on the chrome and glass coffee table before he leaned back.

He smoked his cigarette in silence for a minute, and she began to relax when he didn't seem intent on pouncing. She hadn't realized just how strung-up she was until then.

"That's better," he said, glancing at her. "Now, suppose you tell me what's got you so upset."

She clasped her hands in her lap and stared down at them. "Dennis has accused me of being an unfit mother. He's stating in his custody suit that I'm having an affair with you."

"Well, honey, we knew he was going to, didn't we?" he asked reasonably.

"Yes, but he's done it! It will make headlines, don't you see?" she asked, her eyes wide with apprehension. "Janet will be hurt!"

His face hardened. "You overestimate my mother's capacity for pain."

"And you underestimate it," she countered. "She's a sensitive woman, and her health doesn't seem all that good, Gabe. I don't want to do this to her. Becky's so young, she won't even understand it, but other people will.''

He studied the tip of his cigarette. "It bothers you, what other people think?"

"I know you don't care what they say about you," she muttered. "But I'm not a man."

"Thank God," he drawled. He lifted the cigarette to his mouth and took another draw, stretching lazily. "I'm tired," he said unexpectedly. "I hadn't realized how lazy I've gotten since I've been hanging around the house this past week."

"You, lazy?" She laughed. "That'll be the day."

He draped a long arm across the back of the sofa and stared down at her. The shirt pulled taut across his chest, revealing a patch of dark skin and thick hair at the wide opening. Maggie averted her eyes.

"I like that," he said under his breath. "I like the way you react to me. You can't even hide it. I can see your heart beating from here."

She swallowed a surge of panic. "You're a very attractive man," she said evasively.

"No, not really," he replied. "Just to you, I expect. But as long as that interest is exclusively for me, I won't complain." He finished the cigarette and stretched back toward the arm of the sofa, his powerful body covering almost all of its length except for where Maggie was sitting.

"Did you mean it, what you told Becky?" she asked, turning her head to look at him.

"Of course I meant it," he replied. "She needs a stable environment, a family, a place to grow up without pressure. She can have that here. I can give her damn near anything she wants."

"She loves you," Maggie said gently.

"I know. It's a pretty big responsibility, being loved," he replied, leaning forward to crush out his cigarette. "That's why I was honest with her. There will be bad times; there are in any relationship. She had to choose for herself."

"She's so different around you," Maggie told him, standing up and staring down at him. "She's always been frightened of men. But she's opened up with you. She laughs and plays—she's not the same shy little girl I brought here. And all this has happened in just over a week."

"She wasn't happy," Gabe replied. "She told me. She was afraid her father would take her away from you. Now she's not." He grinned at her. "I told her what I'd do to him if he tried."

She relaxed even more, her weary eyes seeking his. "You told everybody we were getting married."

"Yes, I did, didn't I?" He stretched, easing his back against the arm of the sofa. His pale eyes narrowed, searching her slender body in the colorful dress. "Come here."

She hesitated. He looked...very sexy like that. Dangerously male.

"Come on," he coaxed. "I'll let you play with my chest."

She colored feverishly and glared at him. "Of all the masculine arrogance I've ever seen..."

"You haven't seen anything, yet," he laughed softly. He reached up unexpectedly with his good arm and jerked, landing her squarely on top of him with such delicious force that it winded her. He held her there with both hands on her waist, immobilizing her with devastating ease.

"Let go of me," she muttered, panting as she tried to free herself.

"Stop wiggling, Maggie," he whispered at her ear, "or I'm going to have to do something drastic."

All at once, as her hips came into contact with his, she began to feel what he was talking about. Stiffening, she tried to move away, but he held here there with one large, lean hand at the base of her spine. After a moment her eyes came up to meet his, finding there a wry acknowledgment, and a kind of quiet pride.

"I'm more of a man with you than I've ever been with a woman," he murmured, holding her shocked gaze. "You can arouse me by walking through a room, for God's sake; I don't even have to touch you."

"Isn't that…the normal thing with men?" she asked bitterly.

"Not with me, it isn't," he replied. "I'm thirty-eight. I've reached the age when I have to work up to arousal, as a rule."

She hadn't realized what an intimate turn the conversation had taken until he said that, and she bit her lower lip. It was vaguely flattering to have him admit such a thing, but it added to the subtle doubts she already had about being able to satisfy him. Love play was one thing; it was delicious with him, and she enjoyed it. But love play wasn't sex.

His lean fingers brushed lightly under her ear, making sweet shivers where they touched. "Relax," he whispered. "You're all tensed up. There's no need to be defensive with me. I won't take you like this."

She colored, feeling sixteen again with this devastatingly masculine man. Her fingers pressed lightly against his shoulders as she tried to keep her balance.

"Come on," he coaxed. "Just relax. It won't hurt to let your body go soft against mine, will it?"

"You're..." She hesitated, trying to find the words.

"I'm...?" he teased. He nibbled softly at her earlobe. "I'm aroused? And it embarrasses you to feel it?"

"Yes," she burst out, burying her face in his throat.

His lean hands spread against her back, smoothing her against him with easy, stroking motions. "Give in, honey," he whispered, his voice deep, silky. "Just relax. Lie against me and let me feel your heart beating."

"Gabriel..." Was that her voice, sounding so weak and helpless?

"That's it," he murmured. He could feel the tenseness going out of her, feel her breasts softly cushioned on his hard chest, feel her legs like silk over his. He reached down to the very base of her spine and moved her softly against his hips, loving the surge of pleasure it gave him.

"Oh, you...mustn't!" she cried. Her body felt hot. Blazing hot.

His face nuzzled against hers until he found her

mouth. In the raging silence of the room, the only sounds were her frantic breathing and the slide of cloth on cloth as he brought her even closer and thrust his tongue hungrily into her mouth.

She couldn't breathe, couldn't think, couldn't fight. She gave in all at once, her mind in limbo, her body one long throb of exquisite sensation as his lean hands explored it with a delicious lack of restraint. He touched her in ways he never had before, learning all the soft contours of her body, brushing at her breasts, easing up her dress so he could caress the long, graceful line of her legs.

"Gabriel," she gasped.

He bit her mouth, his teeth tender, his breath warm and smoky on her swollen lips. "I won't hurt you," he whispered, turning her ever so slowly under him. His voice was husky with passion, his body vibrant with it. His mouth drew slowly, passionately, over her parted lips, letting her feel every texture of it.

Her body ached. It was a new sensation, different from the other times he'd kissed and touched her. She felt a kind of throbbing excitement all over, as if her skin were wide-awake and every nerve were being stimulated.

Her eyes opened as his lean hand began to work

at buttons and fastenings, faintly accusing, faintly shy.

"You have a beautiful body," he whispered, tenderly, holding her eyes. "I want to look at it."

Her lips parted. "I'm frightened."

"Yes, I know." He bent and kissed her with exquisite gentleness. "There's no reason to be. We're going to make a little love, that's all. Just the way we did once before."

That relaxed her. Yes, she trusted him. He wouldn't hurt her. He wasn't Dennis.

She looked at his shirt, wishing it were out of her way so she could put her hands on his hair-roughened chest and explore its hardness. Her brows drew together in puzzlement. She'd never wanted to do that with anyone.

"What do you want?" he asked as he began the slow, sweet process of separating her from her dress and slip.

"I...want to touch you," she said dazedly.

A corner of his mouth curved up. "Where?"

She lowered her eyes quickly. "There," she whispered, brushing her fingers over his shirt.

"Take it off, then," he murmured dryly.

She'd never done that before, either, but it wasn't so hard. Her slender finger worked at buttons, struggling them out of buttonholes. Slowly his chest was revealed, all hard muscle and thick black hair and tanned skin. She almost caught her breath at the masculine perfection of it, right down to the firm muscles at his belt.

One of his long legs rested between hers. He shifted her a little, his hands moved, and suddenly she was bare to the hips. She stopped breathing and tried to grab the fabric, but his hands, warm and strong, caught her upper arms and eased her back down.

He shook his head slowly. "None of that," he whispered softly. "You don't have a single reason to be afraid of me, and I'll never give you one. I only want to kiss your breasts, Maggie."

Her face flamed. She never would have imagined that sultry look in his pale-blue eyes, on that hard face. He smiled as he bent his head to her body; then his mouth opened over her whole breast and took it into the moist, warm darkness.

She trembled. Her hands clasped the back of his head, and as the magic worked on her she pulled him slowly closer. Her body began to move helplessly. She arched a little, her hands tugging.

He lifted his head, and she guided his mouth to the other breast, pulling him down with only a little shyness. The feel of his mouth on her was intoxicating. It made her breath come quickly, it made her body throb. She liked it.

His hands swept slowly down the silky length of her body while his mouth moved to her shoulders and back up her throat to her mouth. Insistent now, he divested her smoothly of the rest of her clothing and began to stroke her in the most unexpected and shocking way.

She started to protest, but his mouth slowly overcame hers, his tongue probing deeply, his hands moving again and finding wildly responsive flesh. She moaned sharply, her nails biting into his shoulders. Then she gasped and opened her eyes.

He lifted his dark head to look down at her with eyes that were as possessive as they were observant of all the exposed cream-and-mauve flesh. "What sweet little noises you make, Maggie mine," he whispered, smiling into her eyes as the movement of his hands produced some helpless writhing. "That's it, sweet, just lie back and let me show you. No, don't try to get away. I won't hurt you. I won't hurt you, little one; I know exactly what I'm doing."

And he did. He did! Once, she almost bit through her lower lip as an explosive spasm of pleasure rocked her. Tears sprang to her eyes, and she looked up at him in mute wonder, her body suddenly trembling all over in a fever so hot she couldn't bear it.

He bent and kissed her with exquisite tenderness. "Softly," he whispered. "So softly, Maggie."

The kiss echoed his words, was a tasting of mouths that transcended sexual arousal. There was a reverence in it, an unexpected beauty.

He stood up, every movement slow and calculated, and looked down at her helpless trembling as he stripped off his shirt and removed his boots. He turned, letting her see him as he removed everything else as well.

Her eyes possessed him, devouring all that glorious masculinity in a kind of shocked delight. He was tanned all over, hair-roughened muscle rippling with every movement he made. He took a deep breath at the blatant pleasure in her fixed stare and felt himself bristling with pride.

She didn't protest when he lay down beside her. Her slender hands reached for his face, drawing it down until she could give him her mouth.

She trembled as his hands found her soft body and slowly teased it again into the fierce, throbbing submission he'd won from her before. But this time he didn't draw back. He shifted over her, giving her his full weight for an instant before his forearms caught his weight. His sore arm felt the pressure, but he didn't flinch. His body was aching, throbbing, on fire to bury itself in hers. It was anguish to hold back, to go slow. But he had to. He couldn't frighten her—not now.

His leg coaxed hers to move, to admit the hard shift of his hips against shocked softness. Her eyes opened, and she gasped as the reality of what was going to happen washed over her and brought back all the old fears.

But he sensed that. His hands framed her flushed cheeks, and he kissed her eyelids closed. "God made man and woman to join this way," he whispered. "Not in animal lust, but in exquisite sharing. I want to give you pleasure. Let me have your body. Let me give you mine."

She trembled at the tenderness in his deep voice, at the slow, exquisite probing. "Gabe, I'm... frightened!" she cried, her voice a keening mixture of apprehension and desire.

"I won't hurt you," he breathed. He moved—tenderly—and held her eyes at the same time. "Watch me. That's it, watch me. Feel me, feel my body cherishing yours..."

It was the most incredibly intimate thing she'd ever felt. Never like this with Dennis, who had hurt her and forced her and never taken the slightest

care of her body. But it was Gabe, now, Gabe's
quiet, hard face above her, Gabe's body so warm
and powerful over hers, his skin as hot as her own,
his hips gently moving down, his body...
penetrating!

Her mouth opened, her breath stopped, at the
feel of him. Her eyes mirrored her frank astonish-
ment. It didn't hurt. It didn't hurt at all, it was...
Her eyes closed on a moan. It was...tender and
slow, and he was...filling her...his body, locking,
interlocking, moving, stopping, rising, probing...

His hand moved down her side, his thumb working at the hard nipple on one breast, his mouth
tender on her face, adoring it, cherishing it, while
his body made a miracle of this unexpected intimacy.

He was breathing as roughly as she was, but
every movement was tender, calculated, unselfish.
He smoothed back her damp hair as she trembled
under him, straining upward, her arms holding
him, her voice shaking with tiny, pleasured noises.

"It isn't sex, is it?" he whispered at her ear.

"No," she agreed in a voice high-pitched with
building pleasure. "Oh, Gabe...it's...not!"

His hips moved now in a slow, building rhythm,
his skin gently abrasive against hers, his dampness

clinging to hers, the sofa cushions shifting beneath them with the hard, sharp movements.

"When it…happens," he whispered urgently, "don't…cry out. Bite me, claw me, but don't…cry out, they'll hear us."

"Gabriel." She was weeping, her voice thick with tears she didn't understand. Her body was like a puppet's, manipulated by his, possessed by his. She followed his movements with desperate abandon, blind with pleasure, her nails scoring him, her teeth against his hard shoulder, her tongue tasting his damp, salty flesh.

It was sudden. Like a flash of lightning, like summer hail. All at once, blinding colors came rushing down on her in a hot, sweet flood, and she threw back her head, arched her body in a tension that had to be fatal as it curled up inside her like locked steel. She made a sound she couldn't hear, burying it against his skin, and her body began to echo the sudden feverish, rough motions of his.

Crashing together, she thought in the back of her mind. Crashing together, we'll hurt each other!

Somewhere in the middle of the thought, her body burst into sweet flames. She heard his deep voice, biting back a harsh groan, felt him over her, felt him convulsing. Her mind welcomed the sudden oblivion that washed over her, the sweet pulsing aftermath of something she didn't even understand.

She was damp all over. It was hard to breathe. Her heartbeat was shaking her, like his, and she was so tired. So tired.

Her arms curled around his neck, and she began to kiss him languorously. On his chest, his shoulders, his chin, everywhere she could reach. Brief, adoring kisses that tasted salt and cologne and pure man.

"You made love to me," she whispered. She sounded and felt awed.

"Yes." His hands drew her with him as he shifted onto his back with a heavy, shuddering sigh. "Never like that, Maggie. Never in my life."

"I thought we were going to hurt each other, at the last," she murmured drowsily. "It was so...violent."

"Violence, out of such tenderness," he mused, giving a shaky laugh. "Oh, God, I cherished you," he breathed fervently, crushing her against him. "Cherished you with every part of me!"

She trembled at the emotion in his hard voice, at the feel of him, the scent of him. She clung, nuzzling her face against his with tears staining her cheeks. "I don't mind anymore."

He frowned. "Mind what?"

"If Dennis accuses us of being lovers," she whispered at his ear. "I feel like shouting it to the world, telling everyone what a wonderful lover you are."

He nipped her ear. "My mother would be shocked. She didn't raise me to seduce women in her parlor."

She lifted her head and looked around, dazed. "Oh, my goodness," she faltered, glancing down at him.

"Shocking, isn't it?" he murmured with a smile, looking down at the scattered clothing. He looked back up at her. "Shocking. And good. Right. Like marriage is going to be."

"You don't have to marry me," she began.

"I want to be with you," he said simply. "Night and day. What we've just done is going to color our lives from now on. Lovers are pretty transparent," he added quietly. "I'd lay odds the whole household, except for Becky, will know the minute they see us what we've done together."

"Oh, no," she moaned, hiding her face.

"Don't be embarrassed," he said, smoothing back her thick short hair with a gentle hand. "It isn't proper to be ashamed of something that beautiful. You're my woman now. My wife. I'm going to take care of you and Becky as long as I live.

And you and I are going to build a good life together.''

''It's asking a lot, for you to take on a ready-made family,'' she said softly.

''I like my ready-made family.'' He laughed. ''Becky's a spunky little thing. I'll enjoy being her father. Just as I'll enjoy being a father to our other children,'' he added, tilting her face up to his. ''Do you want that, to have children with me?''

Her eyes widened. It seemed natural, now, to discuss such a thing. She found the thought not at all distasteful and wondered why. She didn't love him. She was attracted to him, she liked him. He didn't love her. He felt a sexual attraction and affection for her. But the way they'd loved...it had felt like loving.

''Yes,'' she said simply. ''I want to have your child.''

The words sounded so profound coming from her lips that he trembled. The involuntary movement of his body shocked him, and he frowned. This was getting out of hand. He'd wanted her; he'd had her. But he still wanted her. And that question about children had been an impulse, not something he'd consciously thought about. But it was exciting to consider making her pregnant. De-

liberately…making her pregnant. His heart began
to shake him.

She saw the look and didn't understand it. Her
eyes searched his curiously.

"Is something wrong?" she asked softly.

"I was thinking about making you pregnant,"
he said, his face growing taut. "It…arouses me."

She smiled delightedly. That must be a good
sign. "I'm still on the pill."

"And I didn't mean I wanted to start a new family tonight," he said, recovering his senses. He
chuckled as he sat up, drawing her next to him.
"We need to get married and get used to each
other before we take that step. Becky will adjust
better if she has us to herself for a while."

Amazing, how perceptive he was. She touched
his face gently. "You were like her, as a child,
weren't you?" she asked. "Shy and alone and a
little sad."

His jaw tensed. "Yes."

"I didn't mean to pry."

He sighed, drawing her palm to his mouth. "I'm
not used to sharing things," he said. "Especially
not emotions. Give me time. I've been a pretty
private person up until now."

"So have I," she confessed. Like caressing fingers, her eyes moved over him with sudden pos-

session. "I never liked looking at him," she said absently, and then flushed when he chuckled.

"I like that scarlet blush," he murmured, drawing her against him. "I'll miss it."

"You sound as if you're planning a cure for it," she teased.

"Oh, when I get through with you, Mrs. Coleman-to-be, you'll be shockproof." He bent his mouth to her ear to whisper something, and she gasped. He took the sound into his mouth, twisting it sensuously, and she gripped his arms with helpless pleasure.

He drew his mouth away, the expression on his face both explicit and reluctant.

"I want to have you again," he said quietly. "But I don't think it's a good idea."

She stared at him, waiting for him to tell her why, the question in her eyes.

He touched her mouth gently with a lean forefinger. "I didn't plan this. I was going to make a little light love to you, but it got out of hand. I wanted everything to be perfect when we married, complete with a wedding night. I've robbed you of that."

"Men aren't supposed to feel guilty about seducing women," she reminded him.

"I feel as if I've seduced a virgin," he whispered, searching her shocked eyes. "And one lapse is all there's going to be, Margaret. I won't take you again until you're wearing my ring. And I think, deep down, you like that."

Deep down, she did. She stared at his hard, craggy face with new eyes. He saw so much that was buried beneath the surface. He seemed to read her thoughts.

"I like very much what you did to me," she whispered. "And I...I'll like it if you...if you do it every night after we marry."

He bent to her mouth, kissing it with soft reverence. "No more fears?"

She shook her head. "How could I ever be afraid, after...that?"

"Because I won't always be that tender," he said matter-of-factly, his eyes quiet and narrow. "Eventually, I'll want you to match my own passion. I'll want something a little wilder and hotter than tonight. This time was expressly for you. I loved it; don't get me wrong. But it isn't what I like."

She colored. "What do you like?"

He searched her eyes. "After we're married, I'll show you."

She felt a little apprehensive then. Would he be demanding? Cruel? Would he want to hurt her?

"Damn it," he snapped, glaring. "Not like...that! For God's sake, I'm talking about love-making, not Oriental torture!"

She bit her lip. "I'm sorry. I know very little about it."

"Yes, I know. I'm sorry, too. I'm so damned hungry!" He turned her, ignoring the twinge of pain in his arm, and jerked her over him so that she was facing him in his lap, her hips pressed blatantly against his. "Feel me," he said in a rough whisper.

Her lips parted. "I don't mind—"

"Well, I do." He lifted her away and got to his feet, bristling with masculine frustration as he jerked up his clothing.

Maggie watched him as she slipped into her own things, admiring the fluid grace of his body as he dressed with deft, sure motions.

"You're very good to look at," she said absently.

"I'm in a temper," he grumbled. "Don't push your luck."

"Why? What will you do?" she teased softly, smiling.

He glared at her. "Do you really want to know?" He leaned down, his shirt unbuttoned, and put his hand on either side of her. With his hair tumbling over his forehead, his mouth swollen, his eyes narrowed, he was so sensuous that she wanted to reach up and kiss that hard mouth senseless.

"Yes," she challenged.

"I'll throw you on the carpet," he whispered with mock fury, "where I'll strip you and ravish you until you scream for help."

"Ravish me how?" she whispered back, her lips parted. "Show me."

His breath caught in his throat. She had potential. There was passion in her. It had been crushed out, but he could revive it. He could make her burn for him. He knew he could.

He bent and rubbed his open mouth against hers in a rough, inciting caress. "Like that," he murmured. "And this." His tongue teased around her lips, probing in quick thrusts until she lifted toward him with a tiny moan.

But he drew back, smiling rakishly. "Next time," he said, watching her, "we'll have to have a radio beside us, to drown you out. You're noisy."

"If I am, it's your fault," she shot back, and laughed. Her hair was in a tangle, her makeup gone, but she was still a dish. "You did all those shocking things to me."

"Were they shocking?" he asked curiously.

She lowered her eyes to his broad, sexy chest. "I felt pleasure. That was shocking," she corrected. "I loved it. Every second of it. I didn't think women were supposed to really enjoy it."

"My God, he was a basket case, wasn't he?" he asked curtly.

"Emotionally, I guess he was. And is. I feel halfway sorry for his wife." She looked up. "He'll hate the idea of Becky being here. He'll fight it with every dirty trick he can find. He was always jealous of you, even though there had never been anything between us. My parents adored you. They were always talking about you."

He smiled. "I liked them, too. Let me worry about your animal of an ex-husband." He pulled her to her feet and held her close to his lean, relaxed body. "You just worry about me."

She slid her arms around his neck. "I want to make love to you," she said with unexpected passion, searching his eyes. "I want to give you as much pleasure as you gave me."

"You did," he said, stunned. "Didn't you know?"

She colored a little. "You were...very quiet."

"I always am," he replied softly. "But I felt it all the same. You felt it just before I did," he added with a gentle smile. "I don't imagine you had the presence of mind to notice what was happening to me. I felt your body shuddering...."

"Don't," she whispered, pressing close.

"It shouldn't embarrass you to talk about it," he said at her ear, smoothing the dress against her back.

"I'll get used to it," she promised. "But it's all so new."

"Yes." Everything seemed to be, with her. He closed his eyes as he rested his cheek against her hair. It smelled of flowers. So did she. Her body was soft and warm, and his began reacting to it all over again.

And this time, when she felt it, she laughed delightedly.

"You witch!" he cried, shocked into laughing himself. "I thought you were too shy to talk about it."

"I'm only shy, not numb," she teased, and moved even closer. "Gabe, I love it when...this happens. I love being a woman."

His chest expanded until he thought it was going to burst. "We'd better say good night before I lose my head again." He lifted his face and searched her eyes. "I'm sorry if I forced this on you. I want to marry you. But I didn't mean to back you into a corner."

She touched his shirt. "Actually it wasn't a corner you backed me into, it was a sofa you laid me down on...."

"Stop that," he murmured darkly, and pinched her.

"You stop it," she returned with pert defiance. "I'm a big girl now, I could have said no if I'd wanted to."

"Bullfeathers," he snorted. "You were half out of your mind. I'm the one who should have—"

"Bullfeathers?" Her eyebrows arched.

He glowered down at her. "Well, there's Becky," he said, glancing away. "I can't very well use my regular words around her, can I?"

Maggie laughed delightedly. He made the sun come out, he made her whole and free and so happy. "Oh, Gabe," she breathed, and embraced him suddenly, holding him, hugging him. "You're wonderful."

He knew instinctively that, like Becky, she avoided physical contact most of the time. The fact that she was relaxed enough with him to initiate it now was devastating. He held her, ignoring the anguish of his body.

"Honey, I'm glad you think so," he murmured against her hair. He smoothed it, admiring its silky texture. His arms contracted gently, and he smiled.

"I never imagined it would feel like that," he said absently, and nuzzled her cheek. "I used to dream about undressing you, touching you. Long after you left here, you'd invade my dreams. I should have realized then…"

"Realized what?" she murmured dreamily.

He stopped, shocking himself with what had popped into his mind. He ignored it, put it away quickly. No, this wasn't going to happen; he wouldn't let it.

"Nothing," he said. "I was just thinking back."

She stared across his broad chest to the window beyond. "Gabe…was it like that with her?"

He stiffened a little. "Her?"

"The woman you were so much in love with."

He drew a quick breath, hesitating. He didn't want to talk about it, to remember it.

"I shouldn't have asked," Maggie said when she realized how personal a question she'd asked him. She lifted her head. "I haven't the right to ask you such questions."

"Haven't you," he replied quietly, "after the intimacy we've just shared?" He touched her face with oddly explorative fingers. "Maggie, it's never been like that with anyone," he said at last. "Not even…with her."

She blossomed in front of his eyes, her face suddenly radiant, unexpectedly beautiful.

He laughed nervously. Imagine, feeling nervous with Maggie. He bent and brushed her mouth with his. "Go to bed. We'll talk again in the morning, in broad daylight. You're very seductive at night, and we've already committed one big blunder, thanks to my sudden lapse."

"It was a very nice sudden lapse," she whispered.

"I thought so, too." He let her go. "Get out of here, will you? This stoic front is going to shatter if you keep looking at me like that."

"One can hope, can't one?" She sighed theatrically, looking at him like a lovesick puppy.

He glared, and she grinned. "Good night," she said pertly, and left him, without even realizing the sudden, sweet difference in her manner. But Gabe noticed. And his eyes began to glow with a soft, budding light. He felt the first tingle of possession.

And it wasn't at all unpleasant.

Chapter Eight

Becky was up at dawn, bouncing on her mother's bed with her dog in her arms. "Wake up, Mama!" she laughed. "Look, the sun's out!"

"Well, tell it to go away," Maggie mumbled, and put the pillow over her head.

"You have to get up!" the little girl persisted.

"Why?" her mother said from under the pillow.

"Because we're going fishing," came a deeply male voice from above her. The covers and pillow were suddenly torn away, leaving Maggie exposed and defenseless in her pale-blue gown, staring up into Gabe's laughing face.

"Fishing?" She gaped at him through sleepy eyes. He was already dressed in jeans and a print shirt, looking fresh and rested and vibrant. And she felt like an oversqueezed cloth.

"Fishing," he replied. "Honey, go downstairs and tell Jennie we all want a big breakfast, then tell your grandma that we'll be leaving before she gets up. Okay?"

"Okay!" Becky jumped down with the puppy clutched tight against her pale-blue shirt and ran off, ponytail flying.

"But I'm so tired," Maggie moaned. Then she came fully awake and realized that she wasn't only tired, she was sore, and knew why, and blushed.

"My, my, no wonder you're tired," he murmured with a devilish grin. He sat down on the bed beside her and leaned over her on his forearms. "Mmm, aren't you a pretty thing when you wake up?" he mused, studying her disheveled dark hair and flushed oval face.

"You're pretty, too," she said, her huge green eyes staring at him admiringly. "Good morning."

"Good morning, sunshine," he teased, and bent to her warm, soft mouth.

There was a new tenderness in him, one that radiated from him like spring sunshine. She sensed it and delighted in it, reaching up to bring his chest down against her breasts.

"That's risky," he whispered at her lips.

"You're barely covered. I can feel you, even through the cloth."

"I can feel you, too," she whispered back, reaching to press her hand over his hard, broad chest. "I wish…"

"You wish what?" he asked gently.

"I wish we were alone on a desert island, just for a few hours," she replied. "And there'd be no one to see us or hear us, and I could be with you the way we were last night."

"Desert islands are in short supply around here," he said with a smile, brushing her hair away from her face. "But I'd like that, too. You're sweet to love."

Her body tingled at the sound of the word, and she remembered how he'd put it, whispering that it wasn't sex at all. And it hadn't been. Sex was just a physical coming together, a brief pleasure. What they'd shared was deeper, somehow. Almost…reverent.

She searched his pale-blue eyes, noticing the tiny lines fanning out from their corners, and the length and thickness of his black lashes. His brows were heavy and dark, and impulsively she ran the tip of her finger over them. It was heady, touching him that way, and he seemed not to mind. His eyes closed.

"Go ahead," he murmured. "Explore me if you want to."

She did. It was exciting, too, to run her fingers over his lean cheeks, the place where his nose had been broken and was the most crooked, the chiseled line of his hard mouth, his stubborn chin. He wasn't handsome—not technically. But he had an inner attractiveness that made his looks irrelevant. And his body was just magnificent, she thought with a sigh.

"I like that," he murmured as she worked her way down to his chest. "I like the way your fingers feel."

"I like touching you," she confessed, finding the realization fascinating. "I've never wanted to touch anyone else," she added vaguely. "It's odd, how I can't seem to stop doing it with you."

His eyes opened, searching hers. "That sounds serious."

"Does it?" She returned his scrutiny. "You don't have to look so worried," she told him, and smiled. "I'm not going to fall madly in love with you and start clinging like ivy."

"That's a relief," he said, saying the words without really meaning them. He grinned. "I'd hate to have a lovesick woman hanging on me all the time."

Her eyes dropped to his chest so that he couldn't see how much his careless remark had hurt. But why should it matter? She didn't care about him. "Well, there's no danger of that," she told him firmly.

He wondered why he felt irritated by her remark. Did he want her to love him? He drew back, a little disturbed.

She looked sad. Her face had lost its lovely color, and she seemed oddly taut.

"Hey," he said gently, tilting her chin up until her eyes met his. "What's wrong?"

"Nothing," she said quickly. "I was just wondering if we should marry…"

"I like you," he said at once. "Don't you like me?"

"Yes!" she said with smiling enthusiasm. "Very much!"

He chuckled. "And together, physically, we create something beautiful and lasting. So why shouldn't friends marry?"

She couldn't think of a single reason why not. There was always the hope that love would come, that he'd learn to care about her; of course there was.

She sighed, watching him, thinking how devastating he was, how masculine and appealing. And he was going to be all hers. No other woman would know him again as she did. He'd be her man. Completely. She felt a wild hunger for possession. She wanted him to wear a ring; she wanted everyone to know that he belonged to her. Her own bold thoughts startled her.

Her green eyes searched his hard face and she thought, I love him. I always have.

She felt the shock to her toes. Yes, she did love him. Otherwise she couldn't have given herself as she had the night before. Especially not when she carried the scars from her first marriage so close to the surface. Why hadn't she realized that before? A purely physical coming together wouldn't—couldn't—have been so profound.

"You're worried," Gabe repeated, frowning.

"No!" She sat up, pushing back her hair, forcing a smile. "Truly I'm not. I just don't know if I remember how to fish!"

"I'll teach you. That, and more," he promised, and bent to touch her mouth carelessly with his.

Maggie gasped at the soft contact. It was suddenly so exquisite to know how she felt and have him touch her. She moaned a little and opened her mouth for him.

He caught his breath at her unexpected submission. His heart began to beat wildly. He lifted his head and looked at her, feeling all man and a yard wide—and frankly hungry.

His lean fingers took hold of the strap of her gown and slowly tugged it down, baring one taut, pretty breast to his glittering eyes.

Her lips parted. Her head fell back. She watched him, glorying in the way he was looking at her, in his obvious hunger for her.

"Touch me there," she whispered huskily.

His heart leapt into his throat. She was going to be a handful. He hadn't expected this. He didn't know what he'd expected anymore. His fingers trailed down her shoulder, her arm. To her ribs, up, but just enough to tantalize. He watched the nipple grow harder and harder at his teasing, heard her breath turning shallow and quick.

"Is it my hands you want, or my mouth?" he whispered, brushing his lips softly against hers.

Her nails gripped his shoulders helplessly. "Anything," she whispered back, her voice shaking. "Anything!"

"Only for a second, then," he breathed, bending slowly. "We can't start something now."

But he wanted to. He cupped her breast in his palm and savored its soft weight as he bent to tease it gently with his lips and tongue and teeth. Maggie was whimpering. The sound excited him almost beyond bearing, but he had to keep his head, he had to be gentle, he had to…God!

He threw her back into the pillows and followed her down, his face hard with passion, his hands pinning her.

"Do it," she challenged. Her eyes were wide and hot, and behind them was the first spark of a blazing need for possession. "Do it. I dare you."

He shook all over with the effort to control it. She was a siren, lying there with her eyes daring him, her body yielded, promising heaven. Becky. Becky would be back any minute.

He eased his grip on her wrists. "Becky," he whispered. "She'll see."

She blinked, as if she hadn't really been lucid. Then she caught her breath as she stared up at him with slowly dawning comprehension. "Oh."

"Oh, indeed." Gabe sat up, drawing her with him, faintly amused even through his own frustration at the look on her face. "I wasn't the only one who got carried away," he insinuated devilishly. "What did you want me to do, for God's sake? Take you right here with the door wide open?"

She went beet red. He made it sound like a quick tumble in the hay, and she hated him for it. She didn't consider that he was frustrated and eaten up with desire. She only knew that he was hurting her.

"Sorry," she said, trying to sound unaffected by it. "I guess I forgot. I'd better get dressed."

He let her go with reluctance and watched her tug up the shoulder strap of her gown. The light had gone out of her, even before she went to her closet and started pulling out jeans and a green print blouse.

He got to his feet slowly and went to stand just behind her, not touching. "Don't draw into a shell," he said gently. "I told you, I'm rusty at this. It...surprised me. That's all."

It had surprised her, too, but she'd only just realized that she was in love with him. And how could she admit that, when he was only marrying her for Becky's sake? He'd said so. The physical magic was a fringe benefit. He didn't love her. He didn't want to love anybody.

She forced herself to act casual and turned with a smile. "It surprised me, too," she confessed, her tone light and superficial. "No harm done."

He searched her eyes. "I didn't mean to hurt your feelings."

"You didn't," she said quickly. Too quickly. "I'll get my clothes on. Where are we going?"

"Down on the pond," he replied. "I keep it stocked with game fish."

"You'll have to bait the hook if you use spring

lizards," she murmured. "I don't mind worms, but I don't like lizards."

"Okay."

She turned, holding her clothes, and stared at him.

He got the message, belatedly. "I'll go see about the gear." He paused at the door and looked back with steady blue eyes. "I won't leave the room after we're married. I don't think married people should be embarrassed to undress in front of each other."

"Neither do I," she agreed calmly. "But we're not married yet."

"We will be by Friday," he told her, and went out the door without another word. And that was the first she'd heard of her wedding date.

She was surprised to learn after breakfast that they were going to fish with cane poles instead of rods and reels.

"What?" she exclaimed, staring at the old, enormously long pole he extended toward her. "You want me to catch a fish with *that?* Where's the safety? Where's the spool? Where's the—"

"It's all one unit, see?" he said reasonably. "Hook, sinker, float, thirty-pound test line and a box of worms. Here."

She took the worms and the pole and gaped at

him. "This ranch is worth a fortune, and you can't afford a spinning reel?"

"I'm not doing it to be cheap," Gabe began.

"A spinning wheel is how you make cotton thread," Becky said importantly, looking up at them. "We learned about that in school."

"No, no, darling, a spinning reel," Maggie told her. "It's a kind of rod and reel that doesn't backlash."

"City slicker." Gabe glowered at Maggie. "What's the matter, can't you catch anything without expensive equipment? I guess you're used to that scented bait, too, and the electronic gadgets that attract the poor old fish—"

"I am not!" she shot back. "I can so catch fish with a cane pole!"

He crossed his arms over his broad chest. "Prove it."

"All right. I will!"

She grabbed the pole and stalked out of the house, off toward the pond that was several hundred yards down the dirt, ranch road.

Becky giggled, holding her own pole over her shoulder as she and Gabe followed at a respectful distance. "Mama never used to get all funny like that," she told Gabe. "She sure is different."

"Yes, isn't she?" Gabe grinned, watching Maggie's straight back as she marched ahead of them.

"Can she fish?" asked Becky.

"I'm not sure," he replied. "I think so. We'll find out, though, won't we, honey?"

"You bet!"

They sat on the banks of the pond for over two hours. When they returned to the house, Becky had a fish. Gabe had a fish. Maggie had wet jeans and a broken line.

"Poor Mama," Becky sighed. "I'm sorry you didn't catch anything."

"She didn't have an expensive rod and reel," Gabe said, straight-faced.

Maggie aimed a kick at his very masculine seat and fell flat on hers when he whirled, anticipating it, and sidestepped.

The look on her face was comical. He grinned and extended a hand to help her up.

"Next time, don't put so much spirit into it," he murmured, delighted at the show of spunk. "You're going to have a hard time sitting down. Again," he added with an innocent glance.

She colored at the insinuation and fell quickly into step beside Becky, ignoring him.

"Isn't this fun?" Becky said, holding up her

stringer of one fish. "Just like a real family. I'm so glad I can stay here."

Gabe glanced at her. "Me too," he said. "It's kind of nice, having my own daughter."

Maggie felt warm at the thought of it. But she knew Dennis, and she was frightened. Gabe was formidable; but what could he do with a man like Dennis, who wouldn't fight fair?

She worried at the problem without finding any resolution. She thought about mentioning it to Gabe but knew he wouldn't listen. He wasn't even taking the custody suit seriously, he was so certain of winning. Maggie wasn't that certain. And she was afraid. Becky was her whole world. She'd do anything to keep Dennis from using her as a key to the trust. Anything!

Gabe made blood-test appointments for himself and Maggie, and the next day, after they left the doctor's office, the couple applied for a license at the county courthouse. Then the waiting began.

Janet helped with the invitations, which were extended by telephone because there wasn't time for anything elaborate.

"It will be fine, dear," she assured Maggie. "We're just inviting some friends from Houston: John Durango and his wife, Madeline. They've been married four years now, and have two boys.

At first they thought their sons would be identical twins, but they're very different. They don't look anything alike.''

''That might be a blessing,'' Maggie commented.

''I agree.'' Janet studied the younger woman. ''Are you and Gabriel going to have children of your own?''

''Yes,'' Maggie said, smiling.

Janet nodded. ''I'll like that. I'll like that very much.'' And she went back to telephoning.

''What do the Durangos do?'' Maggie asked Gabriel the next day just before he left to help finish the branding.

''Do?'' He stared at her. ''Hell, John owns an oil company.''

''Excuse me, I don't read minds very well,'' she muttered, glaring at him.

''Madeline is a mystery writer. She did *The Grinding Tower*, which ran as a miniseries on television,'' he added.

''That was one of my favorite books! You actually know the writer?''

''Well, I guess I do,'' he said. ''She's just a person.''

''She's a writer!''

''Just a person,'' he emphasized, ''with a marvelous talent and a lot of sensitivity. Writing is what she does, not what she is. You'll see what I mean when you meet her.'' He pursed his lips. ''She threw a pie at John and dumped spaghetti on him; she stranded him on a country road with a broken-down car—my God, he was lucky to have survived until she agreed to marry him.''

''Sounds like a rough courtship,'' she remarked.

''It was. He made her pregnant,'' he said softly. ''And she tried to run, thinking that he'd only want her out of misplaced responsibility.''

Her eyes searched his. ''And did he?''

Gabe smiled. ''He'd loved her for years. She didn't know, until then.''

''What a nice ending.''

''They thought so. John's brother, Donald, was sweet on her, but he gave up with good grace, went off to France and married a pretty young artist. They have a daughter now.'' He brushed back her hair with a gentle hand. ''Stay out of the sun. You're getting blistered.''

Maggie made a face at him. ''Look at yourself.''

He grinned. ''Like leather,'' he murmured. ''My skin doesn't burn anymore.''

She wanted to reach up and kiss him, but then she remembered that he didn't want her love. It wasn't going to be a love match. She had to keep that in mind.

He ruffled her hair affectionately. "See you later." And he moved off the porch to light a cigarette, every step vibrant and sure. She loved to watch him walk. He was so graceful. He looked all man, delicious.

She turned with a hard sigh. She had to stop making love to him with her eyes. God forbid he should notice. That wasn't what he wanted from her, after all.

And in the days that followed, it did seem that he wanted nothing more than companionship. The night before they were to be married in a quiet ceremony at the small country church nearby, Maggie was living on her nerves. Gabe hadn't even touched her since the morning he'd taken her and Becky fishing. He'd been roughly affectionate and polite, but nothing more.

"When do the Durangos get here?" she asked him after supper, when Janet had taken Becky upstairs to read a story and Jennie had left.

"In the morning," he told her. "They'll fly up and back the same day. John's in the middle of some financial manipulating. Oil's about hit rock bottom, you know. He's had to diversify pretty quickly."

"Too bad," she murmured. She sipped her coffee, oblivious to the quiet, steady look he was giving her.

"Suppose I lose everything one day," he asked suddenly, leaning back in his chair. "What would you do?"

Her eyebrows shot up. "Get a job, of course."

He burst out laughing. "Always the unexpected." He shook his head. "Get a job. Would you leave me?"

"No, I wouldn't leave you," she said reasonably. "Why should I?"

"Forget it. I suppose I'm thinking out loud." He drained his coffee cup and stood up. "You'd better get some rest. Tomorrow's the big day. Got the rings?"

He'd given them to her the day before, a small diamond and a matching gold band. Nothing fancy at all, and she'd been a little disappointed because he'd only given her the box and walked off without bothering to put the engagement ring on for her.

"Yes," she said, her voice sounding hollow. "I have them."

"You aren't going to back out on me, are you, Maggie?" he asked suddenly, pausing at her chair.

"No." She looked up. "Are you having second thoughts?"

"Not at all. Why?"

"I just wondered," she said, staring at her mauve slacks. "You don't seem to…" She hesitated, glancing up at him. "Well, to want me anymore."

"Not want you!" The words were half-amused, half-angry. "Why?"

She was embarrassed now, shy of him when he looked at her with that vaguely superior, very adult expression on his hard face. What was she supposed to tell him? That since he never made any advances, she'd decided he was regretting his decision? She couldn't!

"Why?" he repeated.

Her face went rigid. "You don't touch me."

"Sure I do," he argued gently. "I touch you all the time."

"Well, not like you did before," she muttered.

"You haven't been all that approachable," he said. "I thought you didn't want it."

She threw up her hands. "Since when did that ever stop you? Weren't you the one who was backing me up against trees when I'd barely gotten here in the first place?"

His eyebrows arched. Maggie in a temper was a new and tantalizing proposition. He tilted his chin up, pursing his lips as he gazed down at her. "My, don't we sound frustrated, though?"

"We aren't frustrated." She threw her napkin down and got to her feet. "I think I'll go to bed."

"So early? It's barely seven o'clock," he remarked with a glance at his watch.

"I'll need plenty of rest to cope with tomorrow," she said, turning.

"Maggie."

She stopped with her back to him. "Yes?"

He moved closer. He didn't touch her, but she could feel the warmth of him behind her. "If you want me to make love to you, all you have to do is tell me. Not even that. Cut your eyes around, smile at me, flirt with me.... Men need a little encouragement. We don't read minds."

"I've done everything except take my clothes off for you," she said through her teeth.

"No, you haven't. You've managed to keep right out of my way all week. I haven't been avoiding you, honey. It's pretty much the other way around."

She drew in a slow breath. He was right. She hadn't realized it, but he was right. "I'm sorry, Gabe," she murmured. "I've been worried—about Dennis, and if we're doing the right thing to marry.... I've been worried about a lot of things."

"Want to talk?" he asked gently.

She nodded without turning her head.

"Come on, then. The cattle can live without me for a while." He caught her hand in his and led her into his study, closing the door behind them. "I won't lock it," he said dryly, letting go of her hand. "Does that make you feel more secure?"

"I'm not afraid of you that way," she told him, surprised that he should think so. "You're nothing like Dennis. I know you won't hurt me."

"I suppose that's something," he said gently. He held her gaze for a long moment, feeling the electricity all the way down to his toes. He laughed because it disturbed him, and he turned away to perch on the edge of his desk and light a cigarette.

He'd cleaned up for supper but was still wearing denims and a green print shirt. He looked very Western, completely masculine, and Maggie's fingers itched to run through his thick black hair.

He was doing his own share of looking at the picture she made in loose mauve slacks and a taupe blouse, both silky and very sensuous. With her short dark hair framing her face and her green eyes wide and soft, she was a vision.

"You look more and more like your mother," he remarked unexpectedly. "She was a beauty, too."

Maggie flushed. "I'm not pretty."

"You are to me," he replied. "I like the way you look."

"Thanks." She sat down on the long leather divan and folded her hands in her lap.

"You wanted to talk," he said, waving his cigarette in her direction. "What about?"

"What if we lose the court case?"

"For God's sake, we aren't going to lose," he said shortly, impatient with her. "I won't let him have Becky."

"If the court says so, we'll have to."

"The court won't say so." He lifted the cigarette to his mouth.

"I can't help worrying." She sighed. "Becky and I have had some hard knocks because of him. She's worried, too."

"Well, I'm not," he told her. "Everything's under control. There's no need to dwell on it."

"That's right, just tell me. Like you tell everybody." She got to her feet, lashing out at him for the first time. "You're Tonto and the Lone Ranger; nothing bothers you, you can beat the world...."

"I can sure as hell try," he agreed, smiling. "Come here, saucy little woman. You're just frustrated, and I can take care of that."

"Oh, can you? How?" she asked with a cold, level stare.

His eyebrows arched. "Ouch," he said. "You want to bite, don't you?"

"I hate men," she muttered, glaring at him.

"I figured it would come out sooner or later. I guess it's a good thing it was sooner." He crushed out his cigarette, slowly and deliberately, and came off the desk into a posture that made her heart race.

"Don't you touch me," she challenged, backing up. "I'm not in the mood to be subdued by the superior male."

"Oh, I think you are," he said with a slow, devilish smile. He moved toward her, holding her eyes, backing her toward the divan she'd vacated. "I think that's exactly what you want—to be shown that I still find you desirable."

"I won't beg for your exclusive attentions!"

"I wouldn't beg for yours, either," he replied easily. "I don't think people need to be put in that position." He stopped when she'd reached the divan and, watching her, began to unbutton his shirt with slow, careless motions of his lean fingers.

"What are you doing now?" she asked breathlessly.

"Getting comfortable," he murmured. "Lie down, Maggie."

"You said we wouldn't...!"

"And we're not going to," he promised. "But I think you need some reassurance. Maybe I need it, too. Marriage is a big step."

"Yes, I know."

"Come on, lie down," he coaxed. He took her by the waist and eased her down onto the wide divan, sitting up long enough to strip off his shirt.

His chest was broad and brown and covered with a thick wedge of hair, and she stared at it helplessly, remembering how it felt to run her hands over it, to experience the touch of it against her breasts. Her lips parted on a wave of remembered pleasure.

He saw that, and something in him began to burst with delight. Her eyes were sultry. He loved the way they devoured him acquisitively. She wanted to touch him. He wanted that, too.

His ribs swelled with a deep breath. "Go ahead," he whispered. "Touch me there."

She didn't need a second invitation. Sitting up, eyes glowing intently, she tangled her fingers in the liberal growth of his chest hair and caught her breath, loving the wiry feel of it, the play of muscles beneath it, the sudden quickness of his breathing.

"You make me burn when you do that," he

whispered above her head. "I don't think you realize how expressive your eyes are when you look at me."

"You have a very sexy chest," she murmured, pressing her hands flat to savor its warm strength.

"I could return the compliment," he said dryly. "You're a sweet sight, too."

His hand had worked its way between them. His knuckles were drawing gently over her collarbone, her shoulder. He ran them slowly down to the soft swell of her breast and farther, to the nipple that grew swiftly hard at the tender abrasion.

"Wouldn't you like to lie against me with your shirt off, Maggie?" he asked at her ear. "And feel my chest against your bare breasts?"

She trembled. He made it sound sinfully delicious. Yes, of course she wanted it; but why did she have to admit it?

He laughed, as if he could read her mind. "Unbutton it," he whispered, moving his hands down to her waist. "It's more exciting if you let me watch you take it off."

It was. She trembled at the impact of his eyes when she let the silky fabric fall from her shoulders. She wasn't wearing anything under it, and he had a delicious view of firm, pink-tipped breasts that were just slightly swollen with passion.

"Like...this?" she whispered, needing reassurance. She felt inadequate; she always had since Dennis's cruel needling. But Gabe wasn't laughing. He reached up, lightly touching one perfect breast, and found it cool and soft and wonderfully responsive.

"I don't know why," he said absently, watching her with a rapt expression that was totally male, "but I've always liked women who were small, like you. Not that you're all that small. But my God, how perfect!"

She felt herself swelling, as much with pride as desire. Her back arched just a little, a helpless response to his voice, his touch.

"I'm going to lift you against me," he said, taking her waist with both hands. "Feel you. Absorb you."

He brushed her against him, watching where they touched, his eyes on the pink flesh that buried itself in the thick dark hairs of his muscular chest.

"How does it feel?" he whispered.

"Exquisite," she whispered back. She arched her spine, letting her head fall back so that she pushed against him.

His hands contracted. "Is this what you want?" he whispered, and bent his head to her shoulders.

"Yes," she sighed, holding his head. "Only...lower."

"Where?" he teased softly. "Tell me."

"You know."

"Tell me, or I won't do it."

"Yes, you will." She laughed, feeling him laugh, too; feeling his mouth go warm and moist down her bare arm, over to her ribs, her waist, and then back up to tease around the very edges of her breasts.

Her breath came in tiny gasps. She was burning up, on fire for him. She moaned.

"Lie down so that I can do it properly," he breathed, easing her onto her back. He knelt beside her, one hand lifting her back, the other cradling her head. And his mouth worked on her, explorative, deliciously thorough. He did things to her with his lips that she'd read about and heard about but had never really experienced. He made her shiver and burn, his mouth fierce and demanding on her warm body, his breath coming as fast as hers.

"Maggie," he whispered. He moved, rising, holding her eyes as his body lowered slowly over hers.

She shivered a little as he approached, because he was fully aroused. "Are we...going to?" she asked helplessly, because if he said so, she would. She couldn't help herself; she already wanted him.

"No," he said softly. "Not until we're married. I just want to feel you."

"You want me," she whispered recklessly. "I know."

"It would be hard to miss," he agreed with pained humor. His mouth explored her nose, her chin. "Open your mouth...."

She did, meeting the probing kiss with headlong delight. She reached up and held him, twisting her mouth under his with blind pleasure. He was all man. He was hers. He was the whole world, and everything in it.

"This," he whispered at her mouth, "is stupid."

"Yes."

"Stop agreeing with me."

She moved under him. "I want to make love with you."

"I want it, too. That's why I've kept my distance," he groaned. "You little fool, it wasn't lack of desire keeping me away, it was just the opposite. I haven't slept all week. I've worked myself half to death to keep my body from aching all the time."

"Oh, my goodness," she said unsteadily, looking into his narrowed blue eyes. "I never realized... Well, Dennis never wanted me, you see. Not really. He had to force it, and because of that, he was cruel.''

"I can't imagine a man not wanting you, Margaret,'' he said gently, looking down at the soft breast cupped in his palm. His thumb caressed it, and she jumped. He glanced up again. "Pleasure?'' he whispered.

"Delicious...'' She laughed, shivering.

"Tomorrow night,'' he said, moving his hips deliberately against hers while he looked at her, "I'll do everything you want me to. We won't sleep at all, and when we do, it will be in each other's arms with nothing between us.''

She caught her breath at the passion in his eyes. "Oh, Gabriel,'' she whispered softly. "I can hardly wait....''

He groaned, getting reluctantly to his feet, and looked down at her with a shudder. "Get your blouse on,'' he said, turning away from the beauty of her. "You're going to be the death of me, Maggie.''

"Oh, I hope not,'' she murmured as she sat up and fastened her blouse, warm all over and delighted with herself. "You can't die before our wedding night.''

He groaned again and shouldered into his shirt,

fastening it before he tucked it back into his jeans. She was standing by the door when he finished.

"Will you please go to bed now?" he asked, joining her. "If you want a husband, that is...."

"I want you," she replied with an impish grin. "You hunk, you," she added, batting her eyelashes.

"For God's sake, Maggie—!" he burst out, exasperated.

"I know, stop it and go to bed. I'm going, I'm going. Turn me out into the cold, a poor little frigid woman...." She was joking about it! It was the first time.

He knew it, too. Tenderly, he bent and kissed her. "You aren't frigid," he whispered. "Tomorrow night, I'll prove it to you beyond a shadow of a doubt. Now, good night!"

He walked past her with a grin, and she floated on up to bed. Things were definitely looking up.

The next morning, Janet and Becky were up at the crack of dawn, helping Maggie get her things together.

She was wearing a silky oyster-white dress with a full skirt, a spray of lily of the valley in her hair and several sprigs woven into a bouquet. It was only going to be a simple affair, but she was excited all the same.

"What are you going to wear?" she asked Gabe in the hall as he went up to start getting his things together.

"Oh, jeans and a sweat shirt..." he began, his eyes laughing at her.

"Gabriel!"

"My gray suit, I guess," he replied. "Will that do?"

"You look very nice in gray," she said, smiling up at him. "You look nice in jeans, too."

He winked at her. His eyes darkened a little as they searched hers. "No second thoughts? No cold feet?"

She shook her head. "None at all. And you?"

"Same here." He lifted her hand and slowly removed the dainty diamond ring from her finger, his expression unreadable.

"What are you doing?" she asked.

"What I should have done when I gave it to you," he replied, disturbed by his guilt. It had bothered him, not making a production about giving her the ring. Now he was going to remedy it.

He slid the ring gently onto her finger and lifted it to his lips. He brushed it softly and looked into her shocked eyes. "That's the way I should have done it, Maggie," he whispered. "That's the way

I meant to do it. I made it feel like a merger, didn't I?''

"I—I didn't mind," she faltered.

"Sure you did. And so did I. It may not be the world's greatest love match, but it's no business arrangement, either." He bent again, probing her lips lightly with his. "Now, go and get dressed, little one. We're going to be invaded by people any minute. Tonight, we'll start where we let off in my study last night."

She smiled against his mouth. "Until tonight!"

He laughed and went upstairs with a quick wink. Maggie stared after him, sighing. It wasn't at all like her first marriage. She wasn't afraid of him. Becky loved him, and he was going to be the ideal husband and father. Only one thing was missing.

If only he could love her...

Chapter Nine

Maggie didn't have time to get cold feet before the wedding. The Durangos showed up early that morning with their toddlers in tow, and she became so involved with company and wedding preparations that it was impossible to brood.

John Durango was huge—a tall, broad-shouldered man with a mustache and thick black hair. His eyes were slate gray, and Madeline was his exact opposite. She was slender and had reddish-gold hair, which she wore long, and pale-green dancing eyes. The boys took after their father but they had Madeline's green eyes, and their parents obviously doted on them.

"This is Edward Donald," Madeline told Maggie, nodding toward a plump little boy in a sailor suit, "and this is Cameron Miles," she added, indicating another son in shorts and a striped shirt. "I guess technically you could say they're twins, but they aren't identical, thank God."

"When do you find time to write?" Maggie asked.

Madeline grinned. "At one in the morning, usually. John and Josito try to spare me by looking after them in the evenings when I'm on deadline, and we have a nanny who comes in when we need her. It works out; I still manage to spend enough time with them. I've cut back on the number of books I write, and that's helped, too."

"Writing must be fascinating work," Maggie mused.

"Motherhood is even more fascinating." She glanced out into the hall, where Gabe was introducing Becky to a charmed John Durango.

"We were shocked and delighted to find out that Gabe was getting married," Madeline remarked, watching the tableau. "John was just his age when we married," she added. "He's forty-three now, and I'm thirty-one. Time does fly, doesn't it?"

"All too fast," Maggie agreed. "Becky loves him."

"Yes. It shows." She turned, searching the younger woman's eyes. "So do you."

Maggie blushed, dropping her eyes. "He doesn't know," she said softly. "He thinks it's for Becky."

Madeline frowned. "Shouldn't you tell him? He might feel the same way."

Maggie shook her head. "He's already said that love isn't something he wants. We're friends. That suits him."

"I thought it suited John and me, too," came the dry reply. "Until one night in a storm I lost my head and said yes instead of no. And just look what happened." She sighed delightfully at her sons. "What a simply beautiful reminder they are." She glanced up. "Sort of like human love tokens, don't you think?"

Maggie laughed. "Yes."

The older woman watched her curiously. "Gabe doesn't say a lot about you, but I gather that you're having a bad time with your ex-husband."

"Really bad," Maggie replied. "He wants my daughter—only because she has a trust."

"Rat," she muttered. "Well, don't you worry. Gabe will take care of him!"

Probably he would, Maggie thought later as she stood beside Gabe in the small church, repeating her wedding vows. She tried not to betray herself by crying, but it was hard. Becky was the flower girl and John Durango, towering over everyone, was best man. Janet served as matron of honor. And a few local people had turned up for the brief ceremony.

Afterward, there was a reception at the ranch and Maggie felt her nerves going raw from all the excitement.

"Calm down, now," John Durango told her as she filled a plate beside him. "All these party animals will go home soon, and you'll have him all to yourself—Edward, stop shoving cake down your brother's shirt!" he called to one of his sons.

"Boys look a bit harder to manage than girls," Maggie commented playfully.

He glanced at her with a charming smile. "Think so? Look what your daughter's doing."

She turned around, and was horrified to find Becky sitting in the middle of the floor with a big green frog in the lap of her taffeta dress. "Becky!" she gasped, her hands going to her mouth.

"Where did she get a frog, for God's sake?" Gabe asked from behind her, staring.

"Oh, I gave it to her," John Durango said nonchalantly. "It was sitting on the porch eating flies, and it looked pretty lonely to me. I thought it needed a friend.''

Gabe glared at him. ''Wait until your sons get to be her age. I know your own fatal weakness, *son*, so look out.''

''You wouldn't,'' John said.

''Oh, wouldn't I?'' Gabe grinned at him.

''Go and take the frog back,'' Madeline told her husband.

''I can't! It would be cruel,'' John muttered. ''Look, she's kissing it.''

''Animal,'' Madeline accused, hitting at him.

''Wait, now,'' Gabe said, holding Madeline back as she started past him. ''Wait a minute.''

''Why?'' she asked.

''I want to see if he changes into something better-looking.''

Maggie gave him a hard look and moved past them to her daughter.

''Isn't he sweet?'' Becky sighed. ''Mr. Durango gave him to me. Do you suppose Cuddles will like him?''

''Your puppy will like him very much, especially with catsup,'' Maggie replied, smiling. ''He'll eat the frog.''

''He won't,'' Becky argued, glaring.

Gabe solved the problem. ''I've got some flies

for him,'' he said, reaching down to take the frog from his new daughter. "You can visit him later.''

"Am I really going to stay with Grannie while you and my mama go on a honeymoon?'' Becky asked Gabe.

He sighed. "Sweetheart, it won't be much of a honeymoon. Just overnight, in fact, but I think Grandma's got a special cartoon movie just for you to watch on the VCR.''

"For me? What is it?''

"Go ask her,'' he said gently.

She jumped up, forgetting the frog. Gabe studied it and Maggie, then grinned as he offered it to her.

"I already have one handsome prince,'' she whispered, reaching up to kiss his chin. "But thanks anyway.''

He smiled at her gently and went off with the frog.

That night, after Madeline and John and all the guests had gone, they drove to Abilene and checked into a luxury hotel, where Gabe had reserved the bridal suite. He carried her across the threshold and stared wickedly at the huge king-size bed.

"That's sure as hell going to beat the sofa in the parlor,'' he told Maggie with a grin. "My back still hurts from it.''

"Maybe there's a vibrator built into this one," she suggested, although she felt a little shy about saying it.

He put her down and went to check. "So there is," he chuckled, and glanced at her with raised eyebrows. "Want to try it?"

She stood in the middle of the room in her demure off-white shirtwaist dress and tried to affect a sophistication she didn't feel. "If you like," she said weakly.

He turned, frowning. In his gray vested suit, Maggie couldn't help admiring him. He looked marvelously handsome. "What's wrong?" he asked, coming over to her. "You aren't afraid of me, surely?"

"No," she replied quickly. She stared at his vest. "We haven't spent a lot of time alone, that's all. It's a little strange, now."

He sighed, taking her by the arms. "I should have thought of that. But I was too afraid of losing my head with you. I guess I went overboard the other way."

"It will all work out, won't it?" she asked, really worried, her eyes wide and soft as they looked up into his.

He searched them, feeling wild shivers of pleasure all over. "Sure it will," he murmured. He drew her closer, loving the exquisite sensation it gave him when he felt her tremble. "I'm going to take a long time with you tonight," he whispered at her lips. "It may not be our first time, but I'll make you think it is."

She reached up to his mouth, felt it move slowly over hers, minty and smoky and softly penetrating. And she trembled because this slow ardor was so much more shattering than violence. Drawing closer, she moved her body against his in a gentle rhythm.

His tall, lean body vibrated at the contact. His breath quickened, and he bent, lifting her, his pale eyes darkening as they searched hers. He carried her to the bed, laid her down and stretched out beside her.

The lights were on but Maggie never noticed. The bed was large enough to give them plenty of room, and they needed it. He was insatiable, his body first over hers, then under it, his hands touching, touching hers, guiding. She learned the warm, hard contours of his powerful, hair-roughened body in a new way, a shockingly bold way that made him laugh and shudder all at once.

"Come on, touch me," he chided when she drew away. He brought her hands back, holding her shocked gaze. "We're married. It's all right."

"I know, but it's new," she whispered. "It's still new."

"I hope it always will be," he whispered back. He smoothed his lips down her body as he spoke and felt the sweet, slow trembling start all over again.

He took an eternity arousing her, until she was moaning and crying and writhing like a wild thing. And then he took her—he was patient even then, despite the storm and fire of it—in a rhythm that was slow and deep and demanding.

Maggie never felt afraid, not even when the tenderness reached a peak that threatened to tear her apart. She felt the mattress shudder beneath them, heard his tortured breathing at her ear. Her nails bit into his back, and she couldn't even help it. She reached up with her legs, catching his hips, holding them, her body arched like a bow. Tears streamed down her cheeks and she trembled uncontrollably, crying out in exquisite anguish as the pleasure slammed into her.

Above her, Gabe was feeling it just as intensely. His voice broke at her ear, his powerful body crushing down on hers, shaking her as it convulsed. His hands on her hips dug in and hurt, but even that was sweet.

She heard him hoarsely whisper her name. And

then he relaxed, his full weight settling damply over her, his heartbeat almost frightening in its heavy, hard quickness.

She touched his hair, exhausted, sated. Part of her, she thought dazedly, loved him until it was pain. Her eyes closed and she drew him even closer, her arms loving.

He felt that surge of possession and it aroused him all over again. He was tired, so tired, but her body was tormenting him with its exquisite softness, its eager submission. He trembled and his hands moved under her hips, lifting them into his again.

"Gabe?" she whispered, stunned.

"Shh," he whispered back. His mouth found hers, tenderly. "Shh, it's all right." He moved, and she trembled. His head lifted, his eyes searching hers. "Is it all right if I do this again?" he whispered softly. "I won't hurt you?"

His consideration made her cry. "Of course you won't," she whispered. She reached up, touching his face, her eyes so filled with emotion that he had to look away.

He didn't want gratitude. That was what this was, he convinced himself. He was saving Becky, he was giving them both a home and security. Maybe she was attracted to him, too; but the rest was all sacrifice and submission. That wasn't at all what he wanted.

When he turned his face back to hers, Maggie saw that the light had died in him. "What is it?" she asked softly. "What do you want that I'm not giving you? You'll have to tell me. I know very little about this."

He lifted his face, hard now, and taut, and looked into her eyes. "I think you know what I want," he said half under his breath. "But part of you is afraid to give it to me."

She searched his eyes slowly. Yes, she knew. He wanted passion. He wanted more than submission. He wanted…this.

She let instinct guide her, forcing down the fear of violence that had consumed her for so many years. She reached out and touched him, stroked him, relishing the feel of his body shuddering against hers.

"I can be anything you want," she whispered. She lifted her hands to his face and tugged. "Anything, Gabriel." Her mouth opened against his, and she thrust her tongue gently inside his mouth, twisting her body up against his in quick, hard advances.

"God!" he cried.

It was the last thing he was capable of saying.

He trembled like a boy, hurting her without meaning to in the violence of passion she aroused in him. He held her, gripped her, took her in as sweetly primitive a way as he'd ever dreamed of doing. And she went with him eagerly, every step of the way, matching the hard, sharp motions of his body, matching the ardent hunger of his mouth, holding him, encouraging him, her soft voice whispering things that drove him out of his mind.

Suddenly everything exploded in a spasm of color and back-breaking pleasure, a convulsion of joy that made him cry out against her, that drowned out the sounds of her own savage ecstasy. He saw, felt, heard, knew nothing except the drumming crash of onrushing oblivion. For the first time in his life, he came close to a faint.

He was staring up at the ceiling when her face blocked it out. She looked down at him with pure pride, smiling into his exhausted face, his faintly surprised pale-blue eyes.

"What an expression," she murmured demurely. "Didn't you think I had it in me?"

"No," he said flatly. He was still trying to breathe.

"Well, now you know, don't you?" She bent and kissed him very gently. "I'm famished," she sighed, stretching lazily, unconscious of his appre-

ciative gaze. "I think I'll order a steak. Do you
want something?"

"Liniment," he groaned. "For my aching
back."

She grinned as she got out of bed. "I'll rub it
for you, later," she offered enticingly.

He sat up, watching her open the suitcase and
take out a gown and peignoir before she waved at
him and disappeared into the bathroom. He felt
poleaxed. He'd expected a nice little night of love-
making and had found himself in bed with a wild-
cat. What a sweet, unexpected surprise. He
watched the door, frowning slightly, and then he
smiled. As marriages went, this one was starting
out well. He rolled over on his back and lit a cigarette, conserving his strength. He felt he was going to need it before morning.

In the bathroom, Maggie was feeling pretty
smug herself. She'd surprised him. Good. Maybe
it would start him thinking. She loved him utterly
and completely. Now all she had to do was show
him, with her own actions. And perhaps, in time,
he'd be able to return her love.

But once they were back at the ranch, Gabe was
caught up in business. Phone calls, out-of-town
trips, a thousand-and-one daily irritations that she
couldn't share or prevent. In business, he was still

like a stranger—all cold, shrewd logic and hard-hitting determination; a real bulldozer.

In bed, everything was wonderful—and it got better all the time. But it seemed to be their only meeting place. And when the custody suit came up in court, Maggie was more nervous than she'd ever been, because she felt alone again.

Becky stayed behind with her grandmother while the adults all met in court for the first time.

"Don't be nervous," Gabe told Maggie quietly. "He won't get her. I promise you, he won't."

But that didn't reassure her. She loved Becky so much. The child had blossomed at the ranch; she was like a different little girl, and she worshiped her new father. She delighted in showing him off to people in town or in Abilene when they went shopping together. And they were like a family, even though Maggie felt more like a housekeeper than a wife. Gabe shared nothing with her except his body. His body was magnificent, and they'd achieved a beautiful peak of pleasure together, but Maggie wanted so much more: she wanted his love. And that seemed to be something he wasn't capable of giving her.

The judge was a woman, black and very beautiful and very young. Maggie's heart sank; she would have felt a little more secure with someone older, perhaps someone with children of her own.

It was just as bad as she'd expected it to be. Worse. Dennis sat beside his attorney, smiling at Maggie with open contempt. His new wife was sitting beside him, more intent on her nail polish than she seemed to be with winning the case. Dennis jabbed her, and she glared at him, blond and beautiful, as she put up the polish and assumed a bored look.

Dennis's attorney accused Maggie of carrying on a long-standing affair with Gabriel Coleman. He added that despite their subsequent marriage, Maggie had been more interested in her own sensual satisfaction than in the welfare of her daughter. He even added a tidbit about Becky's stay in boarding school, which he claimed was obvious evidence that Maggie didn't want her child with her.

Maggie felt sick all over. How like Dennis to twist the truth. She sat there, dying inside, grateful that Janet hadn't been forced to come and hear so many vicious lies.

"Stop looking so terrified," Gabe whispered in her ear, and actually grinned. "It's our turn now. Just listen and you'll find out what we've got on that smiling jackass over there."

She looked up, shocked. Her attorney was on his feet now, a nice elderly man with a voice that carried like that of a Shakespearean actor, deep and rich and authoritative. He had a folder in his hand, which he opened.

"We would like to acquaint the court with Mr. Blaine's most recent activities," he began, glancing at Dennis, who'd just assumed a wary posture. He read from the folder. "On the evening of March 15, he and his…wife…hosted a party that was subsequently joined by two plainclothes policemen. Mr. Blaine and his wife were arrested for possession of cocaine," he added with a bland smile in Dennis's direction. "On the evening of March 18, Mr. and Mrs. Blaine attended a party at a neighboring home. They were observed using cocaine, and participating in a…how shall we put it, Mr. Blaine?" he added, turning toward Dennis. "Orgy?"

"Your Honor," the other attorney broke in, rising, "this is nothing more than a deliberate attempt on the part of the defendant to discredit my client. I feel—"

"I have the arrest record right here, Your Honor," Maggie's attorney said blithely. "Along with a detailed report of Mr. Blaine's activities for the entire month of March, prepared by one of the most respected private detective agencies in Texas.'' He moved forward. ''Your Honor, the defense maintains that Mr. Blaine has no interest in his daughter other than control of a million-dollar trust left for her by her late grandfather. We can show beyond a reasonable doubt that Mr. Blaine is continually in debt, that he gambles, that his amorous activities are not confined to the home, that he uses illegal drugs... In short, we feel that to allow the child to live with him would be nothing less than condemning her to a day-to-day hell!''

''Lies!'' Dennis shot to his feet, pale. ''It's all lies! It's just her, trying to make me look bad!''

Gabe started to get to his own feet, feeling a red-hot urge to tear Dennis apart for what he'd done to Maggie. His own Maggie. But her hand restrained him. He glanced at her and, miraculously, calmed down. He sat but didn't let go of her hand.

''One more outburst, Mr. Blaine, and I'll hold you in contempt of court,'' the judge said with majestic dignity. ''Continue, please, Mr. Parmeter.''

Mr. Parmeter nodded. ''Thank you, Your Honor.'' He put the file folder down. ''Your Honor, my client, Mrs. Coleman, was recently married to Gabriel Coleman. He owns the very successful Coleman Santa Gertrudis Ranch, the C-Bar Cross, just outside Abilene. He is rather well-known in these parts as an honest, responsible, highly respected businessman. He and my client have taken excellent care of the child, Rebecca, and Mr. Coleman is prepared to adopt her—"

"Over my dead body!" Dennis raged.

"Sit down, Mr. Blaine!" the judge said sharply. Dennis sat, glaring at Gabe and Maggie.

"—as soon as the legalities are finalized," Mr. Parmeter continued. "Your Honor, a little girl's only hope of a happy future lies with you. We entrust her fate to your hands."

Mr. Parmeter sat down. Maggie clung to Gabe's hand, her face white with horror.

The judge studied a paper on her bench and then lifted her head, pursed her fingers and studied both sides of her courtroom. "I don't approve of divorce, as a rule," she began. "I prefer it when people try to work things out, especially if children are involved."

Maggie's eyes closed. Here it comes, she thought.

"However," the judge continued, surprising Maggie, "in this case, I can understand very easily why a divorce was necessary. Mr. Blaine—" she looked at the stiff man beside the fluffy blonde

"—having gone over the records provided by the defense, I am certain that remanding Rebecca to your care would be a mistake. Your entire history is one of deception and selfishness and self-indulgence. Once you acquired control of the child's inheritance, and went through it, you would have no more interest in her welfare than you would in a blade of grass.

"Now, I've spoken to Becky," she added, surprising everyone except Gabe and Mr. Parmeter, "and asked her where she thought she'd be happiest." She glanced at Gabriel and smiled. "She told me she wants to live with her new daddy, because he's kinder to her than anyone else in the whole world except her mama."

Gabe bit his lip and looked away. Maggie leaned close to him, her hand clinging to his.

"On the other hand," the judge continued softly, "when I mentioned letting Becky go with her real father, she turned white as a sheet and had hysterics." Her dark eyes narrowed as she looked at a now pale Dennis. "She told me a great deal about you, Mr. Blaine, including some things that she hasn't even told her mother. And you are indeed fortunate that you haven't been charged with child abuse. In fact, if the Colemans would like to press charges against you and pursue them, they would be well within their rights to do so.''

''Oh, hell, I don't want the kid anyway,'' Dennis growled, standing. ''I've got a job offer in South America. We're going down there to live.''

And smuggle drugs, Maggie thought bitterly. It was just his style, and he'd always threatened that it was an easy way to make money. But someday his own deceit would do him in, she felt sure of it.

''Custody is awarded to the Colemans, with my blessing,'' the judge said. ''And due to the circumstances, visitation rights are denied. Case dismissed.''

''She's mine,'' Maggie whispered, and put her arms around Gabe. ''She's mine.''

He stared at her for a long moment. Hers, she'd said. He felt left out, as if he didn't even matter. And there was that blond jackass glaring at him across the room. Suddenly his temper flared again. ''Excuse me, Margaret, I've got something to do.'' He started to stand up, staring at Dennis with an expression that meant trouble.

''No,'' she pleaded gently. ''Please don't.''

''I need to,'' he said between clenched teeth. ''I want to break his damned neck!''

Dennis caught his look and seemed almost to

hear the words, because he grabbed his blond attachment by the arm and half-dragged her out of the courtroom in a faintly comical exit.

"Must read lips," Mr. Parmeter mused dryly as he collected his papers. "Lucky man. I know that look. I've defended it in murder trials," he added with a meaningful glance at Gabe.

"I wouldn't have killed him, exactly," Gabe muttered, glaring after him. "But I'd have enjoyed breaking his arm."

"Good job that detective agency did," Mr. Parmeter said. "I'm glad we could afford it."

"So am I," Gabe told him, shaking the older man's hand. "Thank you."

"Yes, thank you so much," Maggie added fervently, and hugged him.

"My pleasure, and I mean it. Be happy," he told them, winking as he left the courtroom. Maggie stared after him, wondering if he realized how difficult that might be. Gabe had turned to solid ice, and he hardly thawed all the way home. Worst of all, Maggie didn't even understand why.

Janet and Becky were standing on the porch, waiting for them with nervous apprehension.

"We won!" Maggie called out even as she opened the door. "We won!"

Becky burst into tears, running straight toward

them. But it was Gabe she ran to first, and he threw her up in his strong arms, laughing delightedly, hugging her with rough affection.

"How's my girl?" He grinned. "And I do mean my girl."

"I'm fine!" Becky laughed. "Oh, Papa, I knew you'd win!"

He kissed her warmly. Janet came forward to embrace Maggie, who felt oddly left out.

"I'm so happy for you," Janet sighed. "We were so afraid."

"So was I," Maggie murmured. "But Gabe pulled it off. He hired a private detective agency," she added with an accusatory glance at him, "and didn't even tell me. As usual."

He cocked an eyebrow. "You didn't ask."

She turned away. "We won, Becky mine," she said, holding out her arms.

Becky hugged her, too, and planted a happy kiss on her cheek. "I'm so glad I can stay with you and my papa," she sighed against Maggie. "I was scared to death, Mama."

"I know the feeling." She kissed the dark head. "How about some cake? I'm hungry, aren't you?"

"Starved," Becky said, and holding on to her mother's hand on one side, and her grandma's hand on the other, she led them all inside.

That night, Maggie thought it was time she melted the ice between herself and Gabe. He'd hardly looked at her since they'd come home and seemed to draw into himself even more with each passing minute. She couldn't know that her careless remark about Becky being hers now, had cut him to the quick, made him feel used. His old suspicions about why she'd really married him had surfaced, and he was sure she didn't care about him. She'd only wanted him because he could help her keep Becky.

She put on a slinky peach silk negligee after the household had gone to bed, then walked into the bedroom to wait for him. He was a long time coming up: it was well after midnight when she heard his step outside the door.

He opened it, pausing when he saw her draped across the bed in a seductive attitude.

"What is it, payoff time?" he asked with cold sarcasm and a smile she didn't understand. He closed the door with a thud looking dusty and tired and as if he'd worked himself into exhaustion. There were hard lines in his face, around his mouth.

She sat up, blinking. "I don't understand."

"I got Becky for you," he said. "Is this what

you've thought up to reward me? The sacrifice of your body?''

"Gabriel!" she cried, horrified. "It's never been that! Surely you know better!"

"Do I?" He took off his hat and gloves and threw them onto a chair, running an angry hand through his hair. "I need a shower, and some rest." He glanced toward her coldly. "Thanks for the offer, but you're more than welcome. Becky's mine, too, now. I don't need gratitude from you."

He went into the bathroom and locked the door, leaving Maggie shocked and speechless. For a long time she heard nothing but the sound of running water, as she sat quietly on the bed, her mind whirling with unexpected thoughts. Did he really think that she'd sold herself to him, just to enlist his aid in keeping Becky? Apparently he did. Then she remembered what she'd said in court. "Becky's mine." When in fact, Becky was theirs....

She got up and paced the floor, puzzling out what to do, how to convince him. She remembered so many little things, then. His anger on her behalf in court, the careful way he put her feelings first, his gentleness in bed. Maybe he didn't know it, but he'd come to care for her. He had to care: why else would her careless remark have had the power to hurt him? And he thought...he thought she was only using him! It was almost comical, when she was dying of love for him!

But how to convince him of that? She paced some more. The water stopped running. She had only a few seconds left. If she let that cold wall come down between them, she might never be able to get it up again. Gabriel wasn't an easy man to convince.

And then she found the perfect way. The best way. The most loving way. With a tender smile, she went to her jewelry box and took out a small round pillbox. Clutching it in her hand, she turned to face him when he came out of the bathroom with a towel draped around his hips.

His hair was still damp and mussed, falling onto his brow. His face was dark and hard and formidable. When he glared at her, she saw the old Gabe, the intimidating stranger she remembered from her adolescence, the cold man who never seemed to smile. He looked utterly ruthless but she wasn't backing down. She had her spirit back, now that the fear was gone. And he wasn't winning this time.

She held out her hand. "Do you know what these are?" she asked quietly.

He cocked his head a little, his eyes narrowing. "They're your birth control pills."

"That's right."

She went to the trash can and, holding his gaze levelly, dropped them into it.

There, she thought to herself with a primitive kind of triumph. See if that ties in with your theory, big man.

Chapter Ten

Gabe didn't seem able to breathe properly after she'd thrown the pills away. He stood rigidly, watching her.

"What was that all about?" he asked, his tone curt. "Is that some other way of showing your gratitude, telling me that you want my children? Well, you don't have to go that far. You're welcome, is that enough?"

She hesitated, and while she was hesitating, he whipped off the towel and turned to the mirror to blow-dry his hair. He saw her watching him, but he didn't seem to mind.

Her eyes adored him. He was so good to look at. All muscle. All man. She smiled as her possessive gaze traveled from his dryer-blown black hair down to his very shapely masculine feet.

"Take a picture," he muttered, because her look was bothering him. He wished he hadn't taken off the towel. She was going to get a real eyeful in a minute.

She already had, in fact, and her lips pursed in frankly amused delight. "Well, well," she said, folding her arms across her chest, "and I thought you weren't interested."

He glared at her. "Stop that. Women aren't supposed to notice such things."

She grinned. "Then put your clothes back on."

"I'm getting ready for bed." He put down the hair dryer and reached for a comb.

"So I noticed," she commented dryly.

He slammed down the comb and jerked a pair of pajama bottoms out of his drawer. Pulling them on with an economy of movement, he snapped them up with a violent flick of his fingers.

"Prude," she said softly.

He glared at her. "What in hell's gotten into you?"

She moved toward him with a sinuous grace, watching the way his eyes were drawn to her breasts, which were already taut and hard-peaked. The material was so sheer that with the light behind her, he could see right through it. "I want you," she said, smiling demurely. "Doesn't it show?"

"Well, I don't want you," he shot back. "Not this way."

She lifted her eyebrows. "For a man who isn't interested, you sure do have a visible problem."

He actually flushed. "Will you quit!" he cried. "For God's sake, Maggie!"

"Am I embarrassing you?" She clicked her tongue. "Sorry. I thought you wanted me to be a little more aggressive."

"I did. I thought." He scowled at her. His heart was beginning to race. She could see his pulse throb under the dark, hairy mat of his chest. "I don't want gratitude from you. Not when I know that's all you can give me."

There was a deep note in his voice that made her tingle all over. "You sound as if that's not all you want from me," she murmured, smiling gently.

He ran a hand through his thick hair and sighed in angry frustration. "I don't know what I want anymore," he said. "It was all cut-and-dried, wasn't it? We'd get married and keep Becky, and I'd take care of you both. We'd be...friends." He looked up, his eyes possessive, exciting. "But we don't make love like friends, Maggie. What happens to me when I love you…isn't sex. And I don't ever want it to be just physical.'' He took a slow breath, his pale eyes troubled as he looked at her. ''I thought a convenient marriage would be enough. Until today, in court, when you laughed and said that Becky was yours. And I felt like an outsider looking in, like a convenience.''

''I know—now. I didn't mean it that way. I'm sorry I hurt you. Because I did, didn't I?'' she asked gently, and moved toward him, stopping when she could feel the heat and strength of his body. ''And I did it again, today, when I told Janet that you hadn't told me anything about the detective. But it was true. You share nothing with me except your body. You don't want to let me that close.''

His pale eyes narrowed. ''You don't know how close I want you,'' he said huskily, with fierce emotion in his voice. ''You don't have the faintest notion.''

Her lips parted. ''Don't I?'' She slid the peignoir down her arms, watching his eyes fall to it.

''Not sex,'' he bit off.

''It won't be,'' she whispered. ''I promise. Watch me, Gabriel.''

She slid the straps of the gown down her arms,

too, and slowly, seductively, bared her body to his glittering eyes. He started to reach for her automatically, but she held his hands gently at his sides, shaking her head.

"Shh," she whispered. "I...need to show you...that I'm whole again. I think you need the proof."

As he held his breath, her cool hands reached for the snaps of his pajama bottoms and undid them, letting the fabric slide down the length of his powerful, hard-muscled legs. She moved close to him then, just barely touching, letting him feel every texture of her skin as she brushed against him.

"Maggie," he groaned, his eyes closing.

"I want all of you," she said, putting her mouth to his chest, sliding her hands down the warm, smooth silk of his back and hips, around to the hair-roughened skin of his flat stomach and thighs.

He bit back a harsh groan and his muscles convulsed, but he didn't try to stop her.

"Oh, Gabriel," she breathed against his skin, her eyes closed, her hands adoring his body, loving the freedom of touching him as she'd always dreamed of doing, arousing him, giving him everything there was of passion and love in her whole being.

"Let me lie down," he whispered, "before my knees give way."

He went to the bed and stretched out, his body arching in sensual expectation, his eyes open. "Come on," he whispered, his eyes glittering, challenging. "Do it."

She'd invited him once in exactly those words. And now she took the invitation. All the things he'd done to her, she did to him. Exploring. Touching. Drawing the very tips of her fingers over skin so sensitive that he began to make odd, hoarse sounds.

"And you say I'm a noisy lover," she teased at his lips as she smoothed her body completely down the length of his and lay over him. "You're noisy, too."

He looked up into her soft, loving eyes and suddenly didn't need words; suddenly knew. His hands slid to her hips, holding them lightly to him. "That pill…" he whispered. "Did you take it today?"

"No." She smiled. "And if you miss even one—" she bent to his open mouth "—it can be very, very dangerous." She bit his lower lip. "I feel absolutely primitive. I want to bite you all over."

He burst out laughing, although it was a sound

laden with passion and delight. He held her hips. "Sit up," he whispered, daring her. "I'll help you."

"I don't know how," she said.

"Shh." He sat up against the headboard, drawing her over him, facing him, her body close and warm against his as he eased her onto his hips and watched her lips part on a breath as he deepened the contact into stark intimacy.

Her nails drew sensuously against his broad, dark shoulders. She looked into his eyes as she lifted and fell, and trembled a little at the newness of what they were sharing.

"I've never done this deliberately," he whispered. "Knowing that a child could come of it, and not minding."

"Neither have I," she whispered back, catching her breath as she saw the depth of emotion in his eyes. "Becky will...like...having a baby in the house."

His lean hands smoothed her hips down against his. "It may take a while," he told her. "Sometimes it takes months. Years."

She smiled through the building passion. "I'll like that. Won't you?"

He shuddered as she moved again, his fingers biting into her. "Don't. I'll bruise you."

"I don't mind," she whispered at his lips. "I'm not afraid of passion anymore. Not with you."

He took a deep breath. "Tell me this isn't some new way of showing me how grateful you are about Becky," he said, his movements beneath her growing sharper, quicker.

"It isn't," she whispered. She lifted closer, watching his face grow taut at the sensuous brushing. "It's simply a new way…of showing you…how very much I love you," she murmured, and found his mouth, and moved suddenly, sharply.

His mind exploded. He wanted to ask her, to make her say it again. But she was showing him. Her body was telling him everything she felt.

He groaned hoarsely under the flame of her twisting body, and his back threatened to give way as the frenzy of trying to get as close as possible threw it into convulsive spasms. He cried out something he didn't hear because the blood was beating in his ears. He was vaguely aware of her own voice, then the world seemed to go dark and warm and gently trembling around him, and he buried his face in her throat and shuddered.

"I love you," she whispered against his shoulder. She kissed his face, his closed eyes, his warm mouth. "I love you, I love you…."

"Keep saying it," he whispered, his voice weak with exhaustion. "Say it until I die. I want to hear it all the time, all my life."

She smiled against his lips. "You love me, too," she murmured smugly. "You said so. You said so, just before your body went wild. I heard you."

"Said it? God, I screamed it!" He held her closer, wrapping her up, cherishing her. "I didn't even know it, until today. I'd always wanted you, cared about you. But I didn't realize it was love until that blond jackass started telling lies about you, and I wanted to kill him. Because you were my Maggie, and he was hurting you."

She smiled, her heart bursting, on fire with new delights. "I knew it the night after you made love to me on the sofa," she told him. "All at once I realized why I'd let you. I couldn't have done it without loving you."

"I didn't even think about that. I tried not to think of you, it disturbed me so. Every time I went in the living room afterward, I'd see your body lying in exquisite positions on those cushions and I'd bend over with pain."

She laughed, looking into his pale eyes lovingly. "Me too," she confessed.

His hands smoothed over her, his eyes adoring every soft curve. "I thought my legs were going to give way when you threw those pills in the trash can,'' he said dryly.

"Mine almost did,'' she told him. "I could hardly walk by the time I started undressing you. And you just stood there and didn't even protest.'' She cocked her head. "I didn't think you'd let me make love to you like that.''

"I wouldn't have stopped you, no matter what you'd done to me,'' he chuckled. "That was so damned exciting, my heart stopped beating a time or two. I never thought I'd hold off until you stopped torturing me long enough to take me.''

Her eyes widened with delight. "You really didn't mind?''

"Honey, lovemaking is give and take,'' he said gently. "It's as exciting for a man to be aroused as it is for a woman. I don't feel any less a man because I give you that kind of freedom with my body. In fact,'' he added with a wicked laugh, "I feel a lot like a man with his own private harem, intent on his pleasure. I loved it.''

"I'm glad. We'll have to take turns from now on.''

He eased her down onto the bed, his body still locked with hers, and moved over her, resting his weight on his elbows as he looked down into her soft eyes.

"Do you think it could get any better than it just was?" he whispered.

"I don't know," she replied, her voice husky with excitement.

His hips moved experimentally as he bent his dark head. "Let's see."

She closed her eyes with a faint smile. Her arms reached up. Heaven was so close, she could feel it....

The next day, while Becky was playing with the ducks near the small pond, Maggie decided it was time Gabriel heard the truth about his stepfather. Janet had been quiet since the wedding and was already talking about going back to Europe. Gabe hadn't protested; if anything, he'd been even more indifferent to his mother. It was breaking her heart, and Maggie wanted more than anything to help heal the breach between them.

"I want to tell you something," she said softly, lying in his arms under the big oak tree.

"You're pregnant already?" He grinned down at her.

She hit him. "It would be a miracle if I wasn't, after last night. But that's not what I meant." She touched his mouth with gentle fingers. "I want to tell you something. About your stepfather."

His face closed up. Grew hard, as it had in the

time before they married. "I don't want to hear it." He tried to move her aside but she clung.

"No," she said firmly. "You're going to hear me if I have to sit on you!"

His eyebrows arched. "Aren't we daring today?"

"We'll get more daring by the minute, now that we're loved and happy and secure," she returned. "So look out, cowboy, I expect to be a sexy shrew in no time. Now, listen. Your stepfather had cancer. He was dying. Your mother knew that; it's why she didn't leave him when he had his fling with your mercenary little intended."

"He what!" He sat straight up, almost unseating her. "And she never told me?"

"You wouldn't listen, as usual," she said. "She did try."

He drew in a slow breath and let it out again. "Damn. All these years I've blamed her, hated her for shielding him. She said he died of a heart attack."

"Mercifully, he did," she told him. "It was bone cancer, you see. He had very little time to live, and the woman was attentive to him, and he was reliving his youth. And it's just as well that he did," she added firmly, "because the last thing in the world you needed was to be tied to some greedy little girl with dollar signs in her eyes!''

"Amen,'' he said, his voice husky as he looked at his Maggie with exquisite love in his eyes. "I guess I've been blind.''

"You might tell your mother that.''

"And shock her to the back teeth?'' he asked. "She doesn't expect me to be nice to her. I'd hurt her feelings.''

She studied him quietly. "Gabriel.''

He grimaced. "All right. I'll make my peace with her. I can afford to be generous now—what with my new family and all.''

"This part of your new family loves you to distraction,'' she whispered, lifting her lips to his warm mouth. "And would love to prove it to you all over again, if she had the strength.''

He chuckled against her soft lips. "I'll be sure you get two portions of everything at supper.''

"You'd better eat seconds yourself,'' she said, smiling. "I feel primitive again....''

His mouth was moving hungrily over hers when a soft, excited young voice broke through the illusion of privacy they'd created.

"Papa! Mama!'' Becky called them, hands on her hips, looking indignant. "Oh, do stop that, and come quick! The ducks have laid an egg! You have to come and look, it's much more fun than what you're doing. Why people like all that kissing is just beyond me, anyway. Yuck!''

Gabriel got to his feet with his lips compressed, his eyes shimmering, trying not to burst out laughing. Maggie followed suit, biting her lips with the effort to remain sober.

"You bet I'll never kiss any boys," Becky muttered as she turned back to the bushes where the ducks had made a nest. "Not me, no sir. My goodness, you'll give each other germs!"

That did it. They broke up. Gabe took Maggie's hand in his and lifted it to his mouth, laughing against the soft palm. "You contagious little thing, you," he teased as they followed their daughter. "I've already come down with a bad case of you, and I hope never to recover."

"I'll guarantee that you'll be properly reinfected if you try." Maggie pressed close to his side, happier than she'd ever expected to be. Becky was kneeling beside a nest in the brush, her eyes fixed wide and fascinated on two large oval eggs that rested there. Maggie smiled at her daughter. Like the eggs, happiness seemed to be hatching all around them. She glanced up at Gabe's vibrant face and found him watching her, his eyes tender with love.

Something he'd said once came back to her as she glanced toward the flowered pastures that stretched to the wide horizon. Something about the pioneers coming, claiming the new territory in a rage of passion. Her eyes turned toward Gabe, and she felt it all the way to her toes. And she smiled.

If you enjoyed what you just read,
then we've got an offer you can't resist!

Take 2 bestselling love stories FREE!

Plus get a FREE surprise gift!

Clip this page and mail it to The Best of the Best™

IN U.S.A.	IN CANADA
3010 Walden Ave.	P.O. Box 609
P.O. Box 1867	Fort Erie, Ontario
Buffalo, N.Y. 14240-1867	L2A 5X3

YES! Please send me 2 free Best of the Best™ novels and my free surprise gift. Then send me 3 brand-new novels every month, which I will receive months before they're available in stores. In the U.S.A., bill me at the bargain price of $4.24 plus 25¢ delivery per book and applicable sales tax, if any*. In Canada, bill me at the bargain price of $4.74 plus 25¢ delivery per book and applicable taxes**. That's the complete price and a savings of over 10% off the cover prices—what a great deal! I understand that accepting the 2 free books and gift places me under no obligation ever to buy any books. I can always return a shipment and cancel at any time. Even if I never buy another book from The Best of the Best™, the 2 free books and gift are mine to keep forever. So why not take us up on our invitation. You'll be glad you did!

183 MEN CNFK
383 MEN CNFL

Name	(PLEASE PRINT)	
Address	Apt.#	
City	State/Prov.	Zip/Postal Code

* Terms and prices subject to change without notice. Sales tax applicable in N.Y.
** Canadian residents will be charged applicable provincial taxes and GST.
   All orders subject to approval. Offer limited to one per household.
   ® are registered trademarks of Harlequin Enterprises Limited.

BOB99   ©1998 Harlequin Enterprises Limited

DIANA PALMER